MW01136657

BRIGHT
NEW
MURDER
A Plain Jane Mystery

Also by Traci Tyne Hilton

The Plain Jane Mysteries

Good Clean Murder
Dirty Little Murder
Bright New Murder
Health, Wealth and Murder
Spoiled Rotten Murder

The Tillgiven Romantic Mysteries

Hard to Find
Dark and Stormy

The Mitzy Neuhaus Mysteries

Foreclosed
Eminent Domain
Buyer's Remorse
Frozen Assets

To Daniel because you are totally the best.

This is a work of fiction. Any resemblance to actual people or incidences is an unintended coincidence.

Bright New Murder: A Plain Jane Mystery
Proverbs 31 House LLC

Cover Design by Andrew Rothery
Cover Photo by ariwasabi

CHAPTER 1

JANE ADLER SAT ON THE COLD, wet hood of Isaac's car. She leaned away from him, her arms crossed. Their spot on the top of Mount Scott gave them a good view of the city lights. The day's light rain had turned to softly falling snow as night fell.

She was damp, cold, and beyond irritated with her boyfriend.

"If you keep changing your degree, you'll never finish school." The vein in Isaac's temple throbbed, and he flexed his jaw.

"Again: I have not changed my degree. And I'll still graduate this spring even with the extra classes." Jane exhaled slowly. Isaac had only been home a week, and they had already had this argument four times.

"You've changed your degree twice since I met you." Isaac leaned back on his elbows. "It's like you don't want to finish."

"You're exaggerating, and it's not fair. I finished Bible school and I started a bachelor's degree in business. That is not the same thing as changing my degree."

"And now criminal science."

“Yes. I added a couple of criminal science classes to my schedule. As well as French. It’s more work, but I’ll get it all done.”

Isaac leaned over to bump shoulders with Jane. “See, that’s the thing. You don’t even speak the language. How are you going to be a detective in Montreal?”

Jane didn’t answer. She couldn’t say what she was really thinking—that she hoped she *wouldn’t* ever be a detective in Montreal.

“Talk to me, Jane.”

“Why? You only hear what you want to hear.”

“Just help me understand why you’re making it harder to finish. Are you trying to come up with reasons to stay here? To not move to Canada with me?”

“You may not stay there forever.”

Isaac leaned over and brushed her cheek with his lips. “I hope I do. It’s my dream job.” His voice was a low, sexy rumble in his throat.

She pushed him away. “Don’t kiss me while we’re fighting.”

“I haven’t seen you since August.” He tried to set his hand on her knee, but she moved a little. All of his little caresses and kisses were making the inevitable harder for her.

“You saw me yesterday.”

"And we had this same fight yesterday." Isaac turned her gently by the chin and kissed her lips.

Jane froze, a hairsbreadth from his closed eyes and slightly parted mouth. "Then quit bringing it up."

Isaac pulled a small square box out of the pocket of his ski jacket. He set it on the hood of the car, right between them. "I keep bringing it up, because I have something to ask you."

Jane stared at the box.

The box.

The box she had been waiting to see since his last visit home. The box she had been dreaming of since she fell for him at first sight, a year and a half ago. The box every Christian girl hopes to get before she turns twenty-three.

Jane stared at the box and felt sick to her stomach.

"Jane…I want you to marry me. Move to Montreal this spring. Be a professor's wife. Don't ever worry about cleaning, or detecting, or anything ever again. Make Montreal your mission field." He opened the box and held it out to her.

One large diamond, with a swirl of smaller diamonds cascading away from it, down both sides of the ring.

"Say yes." He stroked the back of her head with his strong fingers and pulled her close, his forehead bumping hers. He went for the kiss, but hesitated—a pause that gave Jane the chance she needed to act.

She pushed him away and slid off of the car. “I’m not a prize—not another set of letters to add after your name, Isaac.”

“What? What is wrong with you this week?” Isaac held the ring out to her and cocked an eyebrow.

“Nothing is wrong with *me*. *I’m* doing fine. *I’m* working hard to follow my dream and make a difference in the world.” She took a deep breath. “What’s wrong with *us*? That’s the real question. Neither of us seem willing to admit the obvious.” She stopped. She had to say it, but it felt like something smashed into her heart. “This is not meant to be.” She was too mad to cry, but her whole body shook. Right now, at this moment, she should be slipping that diamond ring on her finger and kissing her fiancé. The man she loved. Not yelling at him. Not…breaking up.

“What do you mean this isn’t meant to be?” He shoved the ring forward. “It’s right here. I’m asking you to marry me. We’ll go have adventures in French Canada. You can keep doing the career student thing. What don’t you like about this?”

“That!” The word felt like a knife in her throat. “That’s what I don’t like! I’m not doing a ‘career student’ thing. I’ve been a key player in successfully solving two murder investigations, and I want to do more of it. I plan on cleaning houses and solving murders for as long as I can, but it’s like you don’t believe me.”

"You wanted to be a missionary too, and you're not doing that anymore." His cocky voice made Jane want to punch him in the face.

"Who says I'm not going to be a missionary?"

"You just did. You said you're going to be a detective."

"Right now. I'm going to be a detective right now."

"And for as long as you can. You *just* said that, Jane. You don't know yourself very well at all, do you?"

"Well, if I don't know myself, then I have no business getting married and moving across the continent, do I? I say no. No. No. I'm turning down your proposal." She clamped her jaw shut and stared at him.

His mouth bobbed open. He shoved the ring box into his pocket. "Fine."

"Fine." She eyed the lone bus stop on top of the hill. Right next to the cemetery. "And I'm taking the bus home."

"Now you're just being stupid. Jane."

Jane yanked her wallet out of her purse. "Don't call." The bus was lumbering up the hill, so she didn't run for it. She didn't want to look like a child, but she did stomp away as fast as she could.

She waited with her back to Isaac.

Merry Christmas to me.

The rank odor of dirty people in the overheated bus combined with her heartache made Jane's gut burn.

After two transfers and an hour and a half of travel, Jane made it the four miles from the hilltop to her apartment. She shoved the door open like it was Isaac and she was pushing him away again. She dropped her purse and her coat in the doorway and threw herself on the couch.

"Look what the cat dragged in!" Jake was sprawled in front of the plug-in electric fireplace. "Trouble in paradise?"

"Shut up." Jane buried her face in a feather pillow. She pressed against it until she couldn't breathe, then she pulled away and punched it.

"Whoa," Jake said. "That's real trouble in paradise."

Gemma padded into the room. She was decked out in leggings and an oversized, hipster ugly Christmas sweater.

Jane stared at it. The image of a cat batting at a tangle of Christmas lights made her want to punch something again, so she hit the pillow a few more times.

"Hey Jane, want some cocoa?"

"Shh. Don't talk to Jane. She's mad," Jake whispered.

"Oh, go home, Jake!" Jane threw the pillow at him. She rolled over and laid her arm across her face.

"What's the matter with her?" Gemma asked.

"Boy trouble, I assume."

Jane curled up like a baby.

"What happened, Jane, didn't he propose?" Gemma rattled in the kitchen, but Jane pressed her arms over her ears.

"Was he going to propose?" Jake raked his hand through his hair. "The plot thickens."

Every word Jake said was like a tap on the head with a ball-peen hammer. Jane wanted to throw more things at him, but she didn't have anything else.

"Was the ring cheap?" Gemma asked.

"He does seem like the kind of guy who would buy a cheap ring, doesn't he?"

Jane squeezed her eyes shut. She had to say something, if only to get them to shut up. "It looked like a very expensive ring."

"But then, it would to you," Jake said. "You're not used to real quality."

Gemma squealed, the sound piercing Jane's skull like a drill.

"Don't get too excited, she didn't say yes."

Jane opened her eyes again. Jake was staring at her, his cheeks slightly flushed, and if she had to bet, she'd say his eyes hinted at actual sympathy.

"What? Never!" Gemma perched on the edge of the couch and stroked Jane's hair.

Jane brushed her hand away.

"She turned him down because the ring was cheap." Jake leaned back again. His face turned brilliant red.

Jane narrowed her eyes. What was his game? He was…embarrassed about his jokes?

"Isaac is her soul mate, Jake. She would never turn him down."

"Soul mate or not, she kicked him to the curb on Christmas night." Jake looked away. "And it was about time."

"What happened, Jane? Don't leave us in the dark like this!" Gemma slid onto the seat, and Jane's hair.

"Ouch." Jane pulled on her hair to free herself.

"It hurts now, like taking off a Band-Aid, but the fresh air will make it heal. That's what my mom always said." Jake was still talking nonsense, but he was staring out the window now, not looking at anyone.

"Shush, Jakey. Let her talk."

"Please. Don't call me 'Jakey.'" He groaned and flopped onto his back. "Anything but 'Jakey.'"

"We talked about the future and he, he just doesn't…" She choked on a sob. Her shoulders shook and hot tears rolled down her cheeks. She couldn't say it. Not yet. Because maybe it was just for tonight. Maybe Isaac would see that he was wrong and come apologize. Maybe he did respect and appreciate what she was trying to do.

"He doesn't love you." Jake cleared his throat.

"He thinks he loves me." Jane wiped her cheeks with her sleeve. "But you're right, I don't believe he really does. He loves the idea of me, but not the actual me."

"And that's not good enough. A husband is supposed to love his wife more than himself. Love her enough to lay his life down for her like Christ laying his life down for us." Jake didn't look away from the window. His voice was a bit husky, almost sincere sounding.

A little sigh escaped from Gemma's slightly parted lips. She stared at Jake with big, moony cow eyes.

Jane sniffled, and held her sleeve to her nose. No point in being ladylike around Jake and Gemma. "You two should go out and let me be miserable. I don't need to ruin this night for you."

Gemma's cheeks flushed a pretty pink. "It is an exciting night."

Jane tried to smile. "I am ruining it. This should be your chance to celebrate all of the hard work. Tomorrow is a big day…"

Gemma slid into her black wool coat.

"It's Christmas night. What are you guys doing hanging out here anyway? Go take Gemma out somewhere nice, Jake. Celebrate everything you guys have accomplished. Make a real date of it without me tagging along."

Jake didn't move. "Sorry. I kissed dating goodbye. You know that."

"Celebrate anyway."

"We'll celebrate after the event. We may have done a lot of work getting ready for the fundraiser, but the real work is all tomorrow." Jake remained perfectly still, as though he were frozen to the rug. "If you're not up to it though, Jane, please be honest. We don't need some sad sack coming around and ruining our fun."

The last hint of sympathy had disappeared from his voice, and it hurt a little. If Gemma and Jake had to stay, flaunting their happy flirtation in front of her, at least they could continue to baby her feelings a little. She flopped back onto the couch. "I'd rather supervise takedown and cleanup of the big fundraiser than stick around this joint by myself."

"That's a good girl, Janey." Jake's unpredictability seemed to be in full swing again, as his voice cracked when he said her name.

She appreciated it.

CHAPTER 2

THE EVENING WAS DARK, like all Portland evenings in winter. Thick pewter clouds that had made a perpetual dusk of the day spewed sleet across the town, making this Boxing Day possibly the ugliest day of the year.

Just perfect.

Jane sat on a stool by the window and watched the sleet slide down the glass in slushy sheets. This was no night for smoothies. But it was too late to worry about that now. Yo-Heaven, the frozen-yogurt smoothie empire Jake had inherited when his father died, was sponsoring a fundraiser for Helping Hands Early Education Center, so smoothies it was. Jake was revealing his New Year's Cookie–flavored smoothies at this evening's event, but…Jane sighed. That would hardly be enough to bring people out in this weather.

She turned her back on the window. The doors were opening in just twenty minutes and everyone was still rushing around, though the place looked perfect to Jane. The Shonley Center had moved them to the smaller banquet room at the last minute. The bad news was that it meant they were stuck at the back of a long, empty hallway. The good news was the room was much smaller, so the event would feel like a success even if it failed to meet their projections.

Jane jumped off the stool and wandered into the kitchen. Technically, she didn't have to work until she directed the volunteers during teardown, but helping was better than sitting.

"Hey, Jane. Any word from Isaac?" Gemma licked the spatula she was holding.

"Shut up, Gemma, jeeze." Phoebe Crawford rolled her eyes. "Jane, toss me that towel."

Jane tossed the towel.

Phoebe rolled it up and smacked Gemma.

"Oh, he'll call. It doesn't matter what you think. He cannot live without her."

Jake walked past with a tray full of smoothie samples. He didn't say a word, but winked as he pushed open the door into the banquet room.

"He's not the only one." Phoebe hefted a big steel bowl onto her hip and carried it away.

"I wish you'd stop asking me about him. I don't know if he'll call or not. He's kind of…I don't know how to put it."

"Sullen? Pouty? Brokenhearted?"

"He's the strong, silent type. He might never call again." Jane traced the faux granite design of the laminate counter with her fingertip. "And that's fine, too. It's not like I'm going to take him back or anything. This was the right decision for us."

"You say that now, but wait until New Year's Eve. You'll change your tune by New Year's."

"Phoebe…do you need a hand with anything?" Jane called out.

"Yeah, out front. Go ask Jake. He's got a huge list to do in the next few minutes."

A tuxedo-clad server pushed his way past Jane.

"Never mind that." Gemma tossed her spatula in a bowl. "You stay here and start washing up. Might as well get some of it done beforehand. I can go help Jake."

Jane carried the bowl to the sink. Gemma was right. It wouldn't hurt to get some of the washing done in advance. And she preferred to leave Gemma and Jake to each other. Two birds with one stone.

"You're a dope," Phoebe said. "Why dump Coach Isaac? Is there a hotter man in this town?"

"He's not *in* this town. Well, he is, but not for long."

"Yeah, that. He does have a lame job. I mean, how much money can a *professor* really make?"

Jane curled her lip up in disgust. It wasn't about the money, or lack of money, or even the location. It was about the lack of…respect.

It was about the lack of *mutual* respect. She had as little interest in being a supportive college wife as he had in being the husband of a private detective, or missionary, or…

That was the other problem. He couldn't see that her two dreams were just as important as his one. But the mutual part, yes, she was as much to blame as he was. She liked having a boyfriend…a handsome, important boyfriend. It had made a good change from no boyfriend at all. But, when it came down to brass tacks and diamond rings…

A sob was working its way up from her heart. She squeezed her eyes shut and held her breath for a minute. Lack of mutual respect aside, she couldn't imagine him not calling today. And not coming by this evening, and not cradling her in his arms so she could rest her head on his shoulder while they watched TV, their fingers laced together, him nuzzling her ear. She turned on the hot water and took a deep breath. He was very nice to have around, but that wasn't the same thing as being the one she was supposed to marry.

Once guests began arriving, the banquet hall filled up fast, and it looked like they ought to have had the large ballroom after all. Jane had to hand it to Jake. He knew his events. She had doubted the kind of draw the local preschool-for-children-of-homeless-families could have, but her heart was warmed to see the hundred or more people jostling each other for a taster cup of smoothies and the chance to donate to needy kids. She hadn't signed on as a server, but she carried trays and filled cups and tossed away the empties anyway.

But she kept thinking she saw Isaac out of the corner of her eye. Every time a dark head appeared to the side of the room, she just knew it was him, come to say they could make it work. That he believed she could do something important and exciting with her life. But even though she turned, every time, it was never him.

About an hour into the event, Jane spotted a man with a big camera on his shoulder following a woman in a red dress with stiff hair. TV news? It seemed likely. Jane sidled up behind the cameraman to listen to the reporter's take on the event.

"The folks inside aren't letting the weather, or the protesters, dampen their enthusiasm for this worthy cause." The reporter's face only moved slightly as she spoke, her eyebrows frozen in a look of mild astonishment.

Protesters?

"Excuse me." A man tugged Jane's elbow. "Will there be real food here tonight?"

"What? Yes, of course." Jane squinted towards the kitchen. Some kind of sandwich-and-salad thing was supposed to be coming out before the night was over. "Just give it a few minutes, okay?" She gave him a quick nod and slid away through the crowd. She opened the door a crack and peered into the hallway.

A dozen hippies and punks and hipsters were gathered in the hall with tattered cardboard signs. The sleet had battered them on their way into the event, but their message was clear. And so was the person in charge.

Rose of Sharon Willis.

The "Helpers" had arrived.

Jane scratched her head. The Human Liberation Party was all about eating right, but what was wrong with smoothies? Or educating homeless preschoolers? Jane slipped out of the door so she could hear better.

Rose of Sharon stood on top of an old-fashioned soapbox, her banged-up red megaphone at her lips. The hubbub in the crowd made it hard to hear, but Jane made out a few choice sentiments.

"We're not baby COWS! We're NOT baby cows! WE'RE not baby cows!" The emphasis was on a different word each time, but the point was clear. Rose of Sharon had a problem with milk. Rose of Sharon turned on her box and seemed to catch Jane's eye. "Are YOU a baby cow?"

Jane wanted to duck and cover, but instead, she shook her head no.

"That's a good girl!" Rose of Sharon spun on her box to call out to a janitor that was passing by.

Jane exhaled slowly. HLP wasn't doing any harm. They hadn't prevented anyone from getting to the fundraiser. Kids would get their preschool, and that's what was important.

Rose of Sharon dragged her soapbox right in front of the door and pushed it open. Megaphone to mouth, she began her favorite protest song. "I like to eat apples and bananas."

Jane sidled through the crowd, but couldn't get past the soapbox. Jake hovered near the door, just on the other side, and she managed to catch his eye.

He pulled a chair up to the doorway and stood eye to eye with Rose of Sharon. "What do you have against the children, Rose? What did they ever do to you?"

Jane was pushed aside as the reporter and her cameraman took her spot near the action.

Rose of Sharon's thin, leathery face was beet red. "Why are you poisoning the children? Why are you using the children to poison the city? We thought you'd learned your lesson, Crawford. We thought you'd changed your ways, but you keep trying to kill us!"

"I'd kill for a hamburger right about now, that's true," Jake said with a smirk that was captured on the reporter's camera. In fact, Jake was turned towards the camera on purpose, as far as Jane could tell.

"You'll kill us all if you don't quit forcing your animal products on our fragile bodies."

Jake cupped his hands around his mouth like he was going to begin his own chant, but Jane shook her head.

Jake shrugged and stepped off of the chair, his eyes narrowed.

Jane managed to wheedle her way through the crowd to Jake.

"I'm not trying to kill people, Jane. Just trying to help out your cousin's charity." Jake lowered his voice.

"I know, Jake, I know." Jane turned to Rose of Sharon. "Listen, Rose, can you take this outside? I don't want to have to call security, but I will if I need to."

"But you're not a baby cow!"

"Of course I'm not, Rose. But…it's not like it's high-fructose corn syrup, right?"

Jake cleared his throat.

"Never mind."

Jane dragged Jake back to the table of smoothie samples. The party had begun to deteriorate.

A red-faced man with a bald head yelled at a younger, taller man in a suit.

A woman with bobbed black hair pushed another woman with bobbed black hair out of her way.

A man in a sweater with leather patches on the sleeves punched one of the hippies holding the door open. Punched him right in the face.

Then a woman screamed.

Jane froze. The room went completely silent.

Jake climbed back on his chair so he could see over the top of the crowd. "Who was that? Does anyone know who that was? Is everyone okay?" His voice had turned serious, manly, and in charge. She had never seen him like that before. Not once. "This event was meant to benefit the most vulnerable children in our community. It was not meant to insult our friends who believe in a different way of eating, or to harm anyone. That scream sounded like someone was really hurt. Everyone look around, and holler if someone near you has been injured."

A low murmur spread across the room, then another woman screamed.

The crowd jumped to life, and Jake pushed his way through the people with Jane right behind him.

A woman in a denim skirt and Christmas sweater knelt beside another woman, who lay on the ground, a pool of blood forming on her sweater.

The woman kneeling on the floor rocked back and forth, sobbing.

Jake checked the pulse of the injured woman. "Jane, call 911."

Jane pressed the phone to her ear and ducked through the crowd. She told them what little she knew: injured, bleeding, unconscious, and where they were located, and then she hung up. She needed to breathe.

The volume in the packed room had gone back to a loud roar. A man in a red-and-green Christmas sweater whose head was just above, and almost directly over, Jane's own kept shouting, "No, let's go home NOW." Jane tried to maneuver around him, but the woman he was shouting at reached for him and caught Jane in her arms.

"Excuse me," Jane whispered.

"Well!" The woman kept a tight grip on the sweater man with one hand, but let Jane go free.

The room had seemed pleasantly full when the party was new, but with everyone jostling to get out but being repulsed by the protesters, and the fear and yelling, it was a bedlam that made Jane's head spin.

"Excuse me!" Rose of Sharon had climbed up on the table full of smoothie samples. "EXCUSE ME!"

The room simmered to a low boil.

"It has come to my attention that someone in this room has been seriously injured. I have taken the responsibility to keep everyone present in the situation. No one has left the room through the main door. The paramedics will be here as soon as they can—any minute. I need everyone to take a seat along the walls, leaving a center aisle through the room to the injured party, do you understand?"

The people seemed to want a leader, and though they murmured in frustration, they shuffled to the sides of the room, and some people even sat down.

"Thank you."

Jane jerked her head up. Rose of Sharon had thanked them?

"In times of crisis, people need to come together and work with their enemies for the greater good. Because we are here protesting, it is of utmost importance that the authorities arrive to a calm scene. Any kind of chaos and my friends and I will be arrested."

"Let them be arrested!" a deep voice from the back of the room interrupted her.

"Yeah!" A throaty female voice joined his.

Jake hopped up on the table with Rose of Sharon, though Jane hadn't seen how he got there. "That's enough. For better or worse, the lady is right. We need to be calm so that the medics can treat the injured woman as quickly as possible. Right now, I'd like to know if someone can tell me who she is."

"I've never seen her before at all!" The speaker was a woman applying pressure to the wound. "Does anyone know this woman?"

Before anyone could answer, four paramedics barreled into the room. They paused in the door just long enough to spot the party they needed to help.

A pair of policemen stationed themselves at the door.

Jake climbed down from the table and joined Jane. He leaned close, his warm breath on her ear. “Now’s your chance, Janey. Someone stabbed that poor woman. But whodunit, and why?”

CHAPTER 3

A SLEW OF PARAMEDICS who seemed in control, but in a hurry, carted the injured woman away on a stretcher. Before Jane had a chance to pull herself together, more police officers poured into the room and began to sort the people into groups for questioning.

Jake joined the officer who looked like he was in charge.

Jane hung off to the side, but near enough to hear. Jake had been right. This was her chance to put her fall criminal justice classes into action—to test her detection skills.

"I had them sort of line up to make room for the paramedics," Jake said.

"That was smart." The officer was an older man, or, somewhat older. He had grey hair, but his face didn't look as old as her dad's did. Maybe he was in his forties? She thought he must be because he had the old-style wire-rimmed glasses with bifocal lines cut into them. No one wore glasses like that anymore. He also wore a trench coat and black slacks. Jane was glad to see her observation skills were working, but she needed to focus on the individuals in the crowd and not on the officer. The officer was the last person to have stabbed the guest. He hadn't even been at the party.

Or had he?

Jane chewed on her lip. Maybe he *was* the killer. After all, he was the very last one she would suspect. And she hadn't seen him come in.

"Didn't I, Jane?" Jake nudged her.

"What? I'm sorry. What did you say?"

"Didn't I give the guest list to Gemma to take care of?"

"Oh, yes. I think you did."

"Why would you do that?" the officer asked.

"The preschool thing is kind of her baby. She's a friend. I saw that I could help her with the refreshments and just putting stuff together, but she had to come up with the potential donors herself. Own it and all that."

The detective nodded. "And did she?"

"Well…" Jake hung his head a little. "Her list was fairly sparse, so I made a few calls. But as far as any formal list goes, she's the one that has it."

"Can you point her out to me?"

Jane scanned the room and spotted her cousin slumped in a corner. Her navy cotton dress was crumpled, and her bobbed hair was a sweaty mess. "She's over there, to the left. With the black hair and blue dress." She pointed Gemma out.

"Thanks. Please try and help keep everyone in the room until we're done getting names and information."

"Of course," Jane said.

When the officer was out of earshot, Jake nudged her again. "Follow him. Listen to everything he says. Where's your notebook?"

"My notebook?"

"You detectives are always supposed to have those long, skinny notebooks. Oh, wait. That's journalists. You aren't a journalist, are you?"

"No. I'm not a journalist."

"Hold tight." Jake ran to the kitchen and back before Jane knew what was happening. "Use this." He handed her a thin tablet.

"What's this for?"

"It's for ease of communication in a modern world, Jane. Now go take notes!" He shoved her forward. If Jane had a dollar for every time he had pushed, shoved, tweaked, or nudged her in the last day, she could buy her own tablet.

She followed the policeman, but tried to keep enough room for another person between him and herself so that he wouldn't notice her.

He started with Gemma.

Jane took that time to figure out how to turn on Jake's tablet and find the note-taking app. By the time she had done that, the policeman was facing her.

"You're Gemma's cousin?"

"Yes, sir." Jane held the tablet by her side, hoping he wouldn't notice.

"I'm Detective Walters. Where were you standing when the woman was stabbed?"

"I was up front when I heard a scream. I think it was her. But I didn't see anything."

"Nothing unusual at all?"

"No. I mean, the protesters had come inside the building and I was really preoccupied. I wanted to try and defuse that situation."

"I see. Can you point out the protesters to me?"

Jane indicated the huddled protesters who made their home against the wall by the door. They sat together, knees up and arms hooked. "Over there. It's the Helpers."

"HLP?" He sniffed. "Of course it is. Okay. I'm going to go speak with Ms. Willis." He walked away without another word.

Jane didn't follow him. Instead she watched two other officers make smaller groups of the people lined against the walls. She had a feeling they were all stating their names and phone numbers, and if they had or hadn't seen anything.

She hadn't cracked a single textbook since Isaac had come home. What a dumb idea that had been. A little extra time spent with Crime Scene Techniques and Principals of Detection (revised American edition with foreword by C. Anderson) would have stood her in good stead right now.

But rather than follow the police around or ask her own questions, Jane found a quiet perch on a stool near the kitchen and took notes on what she observed in the crowd.

She had only taken the Introduction to Criminal Justice class at Portland State, and they had only spent two days discussing private detection—so what? It was two days' more training than she had had when she helped solve the two previous murders. And what she had learned in those two days had been pretty good stuff. The importance of observation, body language, and a little Psych 101 on what liars look like.

Jane leaned over the tablet and tried her hand at observing the crowd.

The clump of people nearest her were almost all finished talking with the police. The last person, a woman with big, sparkly earrings and spikey white hair, was answering questions. Her small body trembled, but she made eye contact with the cop and kept her hands away from her face. She seemed to be telling the truth.

The other people in the crowd were shifting and shuffling. A girl about Jane's age clung to the arm of an older-looking man who was wearing expensive jeans with a sports coat and turtleneck. He kissed the top of the girl's head. Jane couldn't tell if the girl was his date or his daughter. But either way, they looked a little scared, but not guilty.

A motion at the back of the room caught her eye. The small circle of people still waiting to talk to the police looked inward, and down, as though maybe someone had fainted.

"Is there a doctor or a nurse here?" a woman's voice cried out. She sounded like she had laryngitis. A person willing to holler out like that despite her own physical discomfort had too much compassion to stab someone.

One of the protesters broke from her group. "I'm a doctor of naturopathic medicine." She caught the eye of one of the police, who nodded his approval. The small group clustered around the fainter made way for the doctor.

An old man in a tweedy coat lay on the floor. His hair, face, and slacks were grey. The doctor checked his pulse. She nodded, and her face visibly relaxed. The doctor spoke with the people standing around, but Jane couldn't hear what she said. Three women handed over their purses. The doctor stacked them and then raised the man's feet and rested them on the bags. She then sat cross-legged next to the man and held his hand. That simple gesture calmed all of the people around her. It was obvious by the way their shoulders seemed to drop a few inches. Two women in excessively high heels sat down beside her as well. The doctor couldn't have been the person who stabbed the woman.

Jane turned to the next group, the one sitting next to the man who fainted. But they all seemed normal. That seemed to be the trouble with their crowd full of philanthropists and smoothie lovers. They were all either perfectly normal or extra compassionate.

Jane took a deep breath and considered the protesters. Would she call them extra compassionate? They had come out on a dark, cold night to try and convince a crowd of strangers that their bodies were worth better treatment.

She gave each protester a good, long look. Three sort of punk-rock hippies, if there were such a thing, sat at the end of the row. Two of them had liberty spikes and Doc Martens. One of them wore a leather motorcycle jacket with the sleeves ripped off. That person held hands with a woman who could have been someone's grandma. She had on a long, flowered dress and a nubby sweater. The only difference between her and a normal grandma was her long, grey-streaked hair. The ends of her hair brushed the floor where she was sitting.

Then a string of hippies in the classic sense, Birkenstock-wearing, long-haired, dreadlocked, all of that, made up the rest of the row. One of the hippies, a tan young woman with freckles on her nose and dishwater-blonde curls, was pale like she might also faint. She kept shifting her gaze around the room like she was keeping her eye on the police. And while Jane watched her, she let go of the hand of the person next to her, and then clasped it again five times.

Finally, someone who looked guilty.

And yet, the protesters hadn't been farther than two feet from the door the whole evening, so could it have been her?

Jane used Jake's tablet to note the woman's description and how she was acting.

Then she sat down next to the shifty dishwater-blonde protester.

The woman scooted away from Jane.

"Hey." Jane wanted to put her at ease—at just enough ease to answer some questions. "You're looking a little pale. Can I get you something?"

The woman passed her hand over her eyes and shook her head. "No. I-I'm okay."

"You're not fasting in protest, are you?" Jane asked.

"No."

Jane bit her lip. How to draw this woman out? She wished her class on interview techniques was not at the end of the school year.

"You look weak." She turned to the young man sitting to the left of the protester. "Doesn't she look weak?"

"Yeah. She does." The man gave his friend a look of concern. "You should put your head between your knees for a minute."

The woman leaned forward and rested her head on her knees.

"I'm going to get you water, all right?" She counted down the line of protesters. "I'm going to get you all water. And some dairy-free smoothies, okay? We do have some made with almond milk."

When the young man sitting next to the shifty dishwater blonde nodded his approval, Jane went to the kitchen. She filled a tray with vegan smoothies and grabbed a bucket full of water bottles. She passed them out to the protesters and then sat with her suspect.

"I'm Jane."

"Valeria." She pressed her lips together and looked at the ground.

"Are you feeling any better?"

Valeria shook her head.

Jane leaned forward, just a bit, so she could lower her voice. "Do you want to talk?"

Valeria opened her mouth, but the young man next to her wrapped his arm around her knee and interrupted her. "She's okay."

Jane nodded, then reflected, "You feel like she's okay and doesn't need to talk."

"That's right." The man sat back, but his face was still tense.

"What about you? How do you feel?" Jane tried to make eye contact, but Valeria's gaze shifted around the room, until it locked on something just over Jane's shoulder.

Jane turned.

Rose of Sharon stood right behind her, arms crossed, cheeks fiery red.

"Thanks for the waters." Rose of Sharon tapped the bucket with the toe of her moccasin. "I can take care of my friends from here."

Jane didn't move. If she had learned anything in Criminal Justice 101, she had learned that she had to project authority to gain trust. She adjusted her posture, made eye contact with Rose of Sharon, lifting one eyebrow as though she questioned what Rose of Sharon was saying, and smiled, lightly, as though she weren't about to pee her pants from fear and nerves.

"Hey, gang!" Jake flopped his arm around Rose of Sharon's shoulder.

Rose of Sharon shuddered.

"The cops are almost done here. I'm giving out the rest of the sandwiches if any of you are hungry, but in about five minutes we'll have the all clear to go home. Janey, thanks for passing out the waters. Can you help with the sandwiches?"

Jane widened her eyes and tipped her head towards Valeria.

"That's a yes? Great, thanks!" Jake headed to the next group.

Rose of Sharon smirked. "If you have any gluten-free vegan sandwiches, I'm sure we'd all appreciate it."

Jane glanced at Valeria. Her eyes were downcast, but the young man next to her looked triumphant. Jane let out a slow breath and headed to the kitchen. Her first-ever semi-professional investigation and she'd managed to wrest one name. And just a first name at that.

Utterly useless.

Her phone rang while she stacked sandwiches. The ringtone alone told her it was Isaac. She turned her phone off and realized she hadn't written a single thing on Jake's tablet.

CHAPTER 4

THE NEXT MORNING JANE ROSE LATE. She made a pot of coffee and sat at the breakfast bar with her phone for company. In the night, she had had three calls and two texts, all from Isaac. She stared at the phone, but wouldn't read the texts. Wouldn't listen to the messages. If she did, she'd take him back. And she was fairly sure she didn't want to do that.

She nursed her coffee like it was medicine. Last night Jake had driven his sister and Gemma home, leaving Jane to take care of herself. Of course, in general, that's how she liked things. But not so much after a crisis. After a crisis, she liked company. Instead, she had come home alone, and gone to bed before Gemma returned. She hadn't slept much, and was paying for it now with a headache and a strong wish to go back to bed.

She held her cup to her nose, the rich coffee aroma warming her even though it was still too hot to drink. She could hear Gemma stamping around in the bathroom, but hadn't seen her yet. If Gemma felt anything like Jane did, it was probably best they weren't in the same room.

Gemma padded down the hallway and into the kitchen. She was up early, for her, and the dark shadows under her eyes indicated she hadn't slept well.

She clicked the radio on, but the sound was just fuzzy white noise.

Jake ambled out of the bathroom, a toothbrush hanging from his mouth.

Jane set her cup down and tried not to stare. "Uhh…"

Gemma didn't look…guilty. In fact, her face split into a giddy grin as soon as she spotted Jake.

Jake slid onto the stool next to Jane. "Mornin'."

Jane rubbed her eyes. What had Jake done now? Though she had hoped for a Gemma/Jake hookup ever since introducing them, she hadn't seen any signs of…this.

"Morning," Gemma said with a nauseating giggle.

Jake winked.

Jane rested her now-throbbing head on her hand. Flirting. The Gemma/Jake thing had been limited to flirting. She had been fobbing them off on each other for months now, but it hadn't seemed to have taken.

They hadn't really…had they?

Jake's eyes were just as tired as Gemma's, and he had a matching silly grin. His slacks were wrinkly like he had slept in them, and his hair stood up on end. He had clearly woken up here. Jane stared, her mouth slightly ajar.

Jake narrowed his eyes. “I did not have sexual relations with that woman.”

Jane gagged.

Gemma dropped her coffee cup. It hit the linoleum with a thud and splashed coffee all over her legs. “Jeeze, Jake, what’s that about?”

“Look at Jane. She’s thinking horrible things about us right now.”

“Jane, you wouldn’t…” Gemma’s face turned fifteen shades of red.

“I, uh…” She took another drink of her too-hot coffee. “Dang it.” She banged the cup down. “If you aren’t here because you spent the night with my cousin, why are you here?”

“It’s lonely at my house, and you have a very comfortable sofa.”

“Go home.” Jane flicked a paper napkin so it skidded across the breakfast bar.

“I couldn’t abandon two beautiful, vulnerable ladies after our harrowing night. Especially while the killer is still on the loose.”

“Oh, no.” Jane’s heart sank. “She did die then?”

“Indeed. If you weren’t such a sleepyhead, you’d know that. It’s been all over the news this morning.”

“Did they say who she was?” Jane picked up her coffee cup again, but she just held it, and let it warm her hands.

"Nope. She won't be identified until the family has been contacted." Jake held his hand out to Gemma. "Coffee me, please?"

Gemma handed him a mug.

"The game is afoot, Jane, and it's up to you to solve it. What do you do first?"

Jane didn't want to answer him. Especially since she didn't know what to do first. She was inclined to take a long, hot shower and then go back to bed, but she really wasn't going to tell Jake that. "Wait."

"You're going to wait, or I have to wait for your answer?"

"I'm going to wait—and pray."

"No extra points for church answers. I want to hear your game plan." Jake grabbed hold of her shoulders and gave them a vigorous rub. "I'm in your corner, champ."

Jane twisted out of his grip. While the shoulder rub felt good—very good, if she was being honest—the daggers Gemma was shooting at her weren't worth it. "It might sound like a church answer to you, and maybe to Gemma as well, but I don't know what to do next. I don't have enough training or experience, and no one has hired me to investigate. I do feel like I was there at that time on purpose, but that doesn't make the job easy."

"Good. Easy work isn't worth it." Gemma yawned deeply after her bon mot.

"Are you on call today?" Jane changed the subject.

"Yup, and thank goodness. We need to get these babies delivered."

Jake lowered his voice so Jane could just barely hear him. "Don't turn the conversation. I'm here to help you, but I can't stay all day."

Jane groaned. "Then go, Jake. I'll figure out what I need to figure out."

Jake threw himself across the couch. "Okay. You'll do your thing. Gemma and I will do ours. Consider me gone, in the 'interfering in your business' sense, even though I'm technically still here in the 'I'm still in your living room' sense."

Gemma joined him on the couch. "And what is our business today?" She didn't try to suppress her grin.

"We need to talk numbers. Very boring, but important for things like fundraisers and such. I have a feeling if you check the account we set up for donations, you will find that the little murder attempt has made your fundraiser go viral. There are some silver linings here today, my friend."

Gemma slid onto the couch. "That's a good thing, I guess."

"You bet your sweet bippy it's a good thing."

Jane rested her head on her folded arms. Jake was going to do half her work for her, she could tell. But what was he going to do about Gemma? If she had learned anything from her readings on body language, the way that Jake had jumped up from the couch when Gemma let her hand fall on his knee indicated that Jane's assumption that they had gotten up to shenanigans last night was the least likely thing in the world. It looked like the Gemma/Jake thing wasn't going to happen.

And Gemma was going to end up very disappointed.

Despite nervously watching Twitter, the news, and listening to the radio every spare second of the morning, Jane and Gemma didn't hear another word about their murder until well after noon.

Jane had spent the morning cleaning for two clients and trying to ignore that she didn't have any new messages or texts from Isaac.

Gemma had assisted a birth.

By the time they met back at their apartment for a late lunch, they were exhausted.

Jane stretched across the couch with a yogurt. Her shoulders ached. Her morning headache had progressed. Now it felt like a nail piercing her temple. She was starving but couldn't put the effort into anything more than peeling the foil lid off of the plastic cup of Oikos.

Gemma slumped at the breakfast bar, her head in her hands.

There was a tap at the door, and then Jake poked his head in.

Jane groaned.

He plopped a greasy paper bag on the counter next to Gemma. "Lunch. Eat. And listen." He tapped his phone and a newscast turned on.

"*The stabbing at the Yo-Heaven fundraiser for the Helping Hands Early Education Center on December twenty-sixth turned a yo-heavenly night into hell for everyone at the party. It is being called a coldhearted fro-yo murder.*

An hour into an event intended to provide quality early intervention education to the children of homeless families, a woman, now identified as Nevada resident Michelle White, was stabbed in the side. The wound proved to be fatal.

White, a mother of one and grandmother of three, was in town for the holiday.

The police believe the incident was a random act of violence."

"It says something about the Adler-Crawford Detective Agency that the latest information on our current case comes from the Mount Hood Community College School of Journalism podcast, doesn't it?" Jake said.

Gemma snickered. "The Adler-Crawford Detective Agency? We're all in business together now?"

"You're not a detective, Gem, sorry." Jake sat on Jane's legs. "Jane, what are you going to do now that the 'Pod-vocate' has handed you your information on a silver platter?"

"I'm going to eat a hamburger. That's what you have in the bag over there, isn't it? A burger with a roly-poly bun?"

"Indeed."

"Then pass that on a silver platter."

Gemma tossed a paper-wrapped burger to Jane.

"You're trying to pester me into action, Jake, but you don't have to." Jane took a huge bite of the juicy burger on the fat bun.

"She has been working on this." Gemma grabbed a French fry. "Not McDonalds, but it will do."

Jane swallowed. "I've got alerts set. I would have heard this as soon as I checked them. And I know exactly what I'll do next."

"If you say you're going to google Michelle White from Nevada, you're a big dork."

"True, the first step has changed. Michelle White is not the Hortense Swiggenbotham kind of name I had been hoping for. But that doesn't mean I don't know what I'm doing next."

"Okay then, what are you doing next?"

"I'm going to…" Jane bit her lip. She couldn't let Jake know she was making this up just now. "I'm going to find out who brought Michelle White to the fundraiser."

"And how are you going to do that?"

"Facebook." Jane grabbed her phone from the coffee table and logged onto Plain Jane's Good Clean Houses Facebook business page.

"Hey guys! I'm looking for the person who brought Michelle White to Gemma's fundraiser! All tips welcome! She clicked the boost button and added twenty dollars to the fund. Then she shared it on her private page too.

"Facebook?" Jake scowled. "That's not hard-boiled detecting."

"Very true. But do I look like a hard-boiled detective?" Jane pulled the elastic out of her ponytail and let her hair fall over her shoulders.

"Fair enough. But you're not going to just sit and wait for someone to contact you, are you?"

Her phone bleeped.

She raised an eyebrow and smiled, but her heart thumped. She read the PM out loud. "*Hey Jane! My mom brought Michelle with her! We can't even believe she's gone. Everyone at home is totally crushed, but I know Mom would talk to you, if you wanted to.*" Jane grinned. "And now, my next step will be connecting with Sarah Henry's mom." She tapped out her request for Sarah's mom's digits.

Jake frowned. "That's all well and good, but I think there should be more trench coats and magnifying glasses involved."

"Don't jump ahead. We'll take this investigation one step at a time."

"We?" Gemma interjected.

"Of course 'we.' I'll need all the help I can get."

Gemma squeezed herself between the arm of the couch and Jake. "Awesome."

Jane got up. "I'm beat. I didn't sleep well last night. I'm hoping Sasha Henry will be able to see me later today, so I'm going to take a quick nap and then a shower. You two…sort out your guest list, and donations and stuff, and then figure out who was at the party that really shouldn't have been there."

"Yes, ma'am!" Gemma's smile could have lit the room.

"Let me know if you need help napping. I'm great with a snuggle." Jake tipped his head at Jane as she walked away.

Jane tried her best to sleep—a fifteen-minute power nap would make a world of difference—but her mind was racing and she couldn't slow it down.

Michelle wasn't from around here. Michelle was a friend of one of her own mom's friends. Michelle had grandkids. But what had Michelle done to make someone want to kill her? Her husband hadn't been mentioned. Was she married? Divorced? Widowed?

Jane sat up and started writing her questions down. First she had to figure out what she needed to know, then she had to figure out how to get the information from Sasha Henry without coming across as nosy, or morbid.

She narrowed her field of questions to learning Michelle's backstory, and learning what her plans in Portland were. She hoped that by comparing the two, she might be able to spot the thing that made her a likely victim.

This random act of violence business didn't fly with Jane. Not at all.

CHAPTER 5

SASHA HENRY PHONED while Jane was still in the shower, a fact Jake used to his advantage.

"My eyes are closed, I promise."

"GET OUT!" Jane poked her head around the shower curtain but held it against herself with an iron grip.

"Trust me, you want this interruption. Maybe not as much as I do, but you want it." He held up her phone and waggled it a little.

"Jake." Jane took a deep breath. "Get out of my bathroom."

"It's the Henry woman, but if you don't want to talk to her, I can."

Jane shut off her water. "I think I hate you." She reached for the phone with one hand, but kept the shower curtain tight in her hand.

Jake pulled the phone back, just a tad.

Jane gritted her teeth.

"Kidding." Jake set the phone on the bathroom counter and left, shutting the bathroom door behind him.

"Sasha? This is Jane Adler. Thanks for returning my call."

"Not at all. You're Nancy Adler's girl? The one who cleans houses?"

"Yes, that's me." Jane sat on the edge of the bathtub, shivering. Her towel hung from the hook on the door, but she was afraid of messing up the phone call, so she didn't grab it.

"What can I do for you?" Sasha's voice was raspy and emotional. "You said you wanted to talk about Michelle?"

"I do, if you don't mind." Jane had a reason for the conversation all lined up, but a twinge of guilt struck her as she was about to say it. It was mostly a lie. "I, uh..." She couldn't do it. She just couldn't lie. "I am a criminal justice student, and I'm hoping to help with the investigation of this case." She took a deep breath. "I don't want to make you uncomfortable, but if you are willing to talk to me, I'd appreciate it so much." An overwhelming sense of foolishness, exacerbated by her cold, wet, and naked state, replaced the feeling of guilt.

"A student? Would this be for a school project?" There was more than a hint of disgust in Sasha's voice.

"Oh, no. Not at all. But...I was there that night, you see. And my cousin and one of my best friends put on the event, so all of us are really...affected by it. Since I'm learning how to investigate crimes, it seemed like talking to you might sort of help us all as we processed what happened."

"I see." The disgusted tone was gone, but all that was left was a weariness.

"Are you free to meet for coffee?" Jane crossed her fingers.

"Why don't you come by and see me around seven?"

"That would be fine. Thank you so much for taking a little time for me." Jane exhaled slowly. Maybe when she was a real detective, this would be easier. She got Sasha's address and let her go. She had enough time to make a casserole for the funeral, if she ran straight to the store.

When she got back from the store, she assembled the casserole ingredients. Rice, frozen vegetables, pregrated cheese, cans of soup, croutons, a bag of frozen chicken breasts. She could make something with this, surely.

She dug around in her cupboards for a big glass dish like her mom used for casseroles, but they didn't seem to have one. They did have a big soup pot though, so she grabbed it.

The rice and soup part made sense, just put the soup in the pot and then throw the rice in.

She stared at the bag. How much rice? Maybe the whole bag? She weighed it in her hand. It felt kind of heavy. Maybe just, like, one can of rice. She dumped the two cans of cream of mushroom soup in the pot and then added a canful of rice. Frozen veg was easy. Just dump it in with the rice.

The chicken was a problem. The chicken breasts were frozen solid and she couldn't cut them.

She got a bigger knife.

She leaned with all her weight on the butcher knife and managed to cut the chicken breast in half. Maybe the microwave would help. She put the whole sack of frozen chicken breasts in to defrost for two minutes.

"Making dinner?" Gemma came out of her bedroom and joined Jane in the kitchen.

Jane took a deep breath. She had so much she ought to say to Gemma, but until a better moment came, she needed to stick to the mundane. "It's for Michelle White's funeral."

"Will there be extra?"

"Probably not." The microwave beeped, so Jane took the chicken out. It wasn't floppy like it was supposed to be, but it was softer and easier to cut. She cut three of the chicken breasts into little squares and dumped them in the pot. She stirred it, and then dumped the whole bag of grated cheese into it.

"What is for dinner then?"

"I'm not your mommy." Jane opened the bag of croutons and poured them on the casserole, too. She stuck the pot in the oven, handle towards the door, so it would be easier to take out when it was done. She checked the clock…the Henrys lived across town, on the west side. If she calculated for traffic, she would need…shoot. She turned the stove up to five hundred degrees. That should get it cooked in time for her to leave.

"I think it's your turn." Gemma pulled off her elastic headband and ran her fingers through her bobbed hair.

"To make dinner? Since when do we take turns making dinner?"

"I made dinner for you last Sunday," Gemma said.

"Take-and-bake pizza. If you can wait until I get home, I'll bring you one." Jane chewed her bottom lip. She should give herself an hour to get there. Highway 26 was always a disaster during rush hour. She clicked the stove up to 515. She didn't have time to mess around.

"You know what we could do…" There was a mischievous lilt in Gemma's voice. Jane decided to ignore it. "We could order in." Gemma winked and dialed her phone.

Jane sat at the breakfast bar drumming her fingers. If a casserole took, what…an hour, at a normal temperature, surely at 515, hers would be done in half an hour? Half an hour was more than enough time. She could even get lost on her way.

The timer went off for the casserole.

Jane looked up from her computer. She'd just check one more thing, then take it out. She sniffed. It didn't smell like she thought it would.

While considering what the smell reminded her of, the front door popped open.

"Ladies. I don't do this for just anyone, I want you to know. And I have to say, I don't think hamburgers twice a day is good for you." Jake set a recycled-paper drinks carrier on the counter next to Jane. "So I brought the New Year's Cookie smoothies—or as the media has been calling them, the smoothies of death."

"They have not, Jake." Gemma rolled her eyes.

"They will. Anyway, I threw in some extra protein powders and some powdered veg. A meal in a cup."

"Gem…" Jane sipped her drink. "You 'ordered' dinner from Jake?"

Gemma shrugged. "All our munchies needs, just a text message away."

"What stinks in here?" Jake asked.

"My attitude." Jane sighed. "Roommates are always a challenge."

"What you need is a husband. They're easy as smoothies."

"Easy as the smoothies of death? Sign me up." Jane took a deep breath. "Wait, I smell it, too. What is that?"

"It smells like someone doesn't know how to cook." Jake picked up a soup can. "Do you know how much MSG is in these?"

"I don't know how to cook. But how can casserole smell like that?" Jane gagged. She wouldn't want to eat a dinner that smelled like a burnt tire, much less give it to someone for a funeral.

"Casseroles can't smell like that. Why are you cooking a casserole at five hundred and fifteen degrees? Are you trying to burn your house down?" Jake clicked the light on to see inside the stove. "Oh, Jane. Really?"

"What?"

"Plastic handles in a really hot oven? For a casserole?"

Jane exhaled through tight lips, making a *pffft* sound. "So, that's not right?"

"It's a wonder you didn't kill us all when we were living together."

"We were not 'living together,' Jake."

"Potatoes, potahtoes." Jake turned the oven off. "Just leave it there until the tenth of never. Don't open it. Don't touch it. Trust me. You don't want to open that oven."

Jane reached around him and pulled the oven open. Smokey, burnt-plastic air enveloped her.

"You don't like to listen, do you?"

"I can't have it start on fire." She grabbed a dishrag for each hand and yanked the pot out. One hand sizzled, since the dishrag was wet. The other hand squeezed the hot plastic handle like it was Play-Doh. "Ouch!" She dropped the pan. Hot "casserole" spilled across the floor and splattered the cupboard doors, and her pants.

She kicked the pan.

"Calm down, champ. Spilled milk's not worth crying over."

"It's not milk. It's goodwill to soften my contact toward me, and a pan I ruined." Jane leaned back against the sink and looked at her mess.

"Well, at least you didn't let it catch fire." Jake jumped onto the counter and sat like it was a stool. "How do you clean a mess like this, Jane Adler, professional housecleaner?"

Gemma leaned on her elbows next to Jake. "Yeah, how do you clean that?" She sipped her smoothie. "Yumm. Thanks."

"Someone appreciates me around here."

Gemma bumped his elbow with hers.

Jake jumped off the counter again. "You're running out of time, Janey. I'll clean that mess up, and you can change into something less toxic."

Jane looked from the mess to Jake and back again. He was right—a thing she was getting a little sick of—she didn't have time to clean up the chunks of chicken, and rice, and soup, and everything else, and still make it to the Henry house for her first-ever intentional investigation.

Ten minutes later—how had the soupy mix gotten into her hair?—she was ready to go. Bleachy rags and tuition fees hadn't been good to her wardrobe, but she had a button-down shirt that still had all of its buttons and a pair of jeans with only two bleach splatters down by the ankle. She looked, if not professional, at least tidy.

The kitchen was spotless, and so was Jake. She didn't want to get caught up in one of his lengthy, rambling conversations, so she just waved as she left.

He followed her.

"Safety in numbers, Jane. I don't want to hear a word against it."

Jane didn't speak. She let herself into her car and smacked the lock button so he couldn't join her.

He knocked on the window. "Plus," he exaggerated the shape of his words though she could hear him just fine, "you told her you wanted to help us all come to terms with what happened. Doesn't make sense for you to go alone." He lifted his eyebrow.

She turned the key. Her engine growled into life.

"And, if you back out, you'll run over my foot." He pointed down.

Apparently he had stuck his foot under her front wheel. She was tempted to drive anyway.

"If the Henrys slit your throat and toss you in the Willamette, I could never forgive myself."

Jane counted to ten. Again, he had a point. Not that she didn't trust the mom of a Facebook friend she had never met, but knew because someone else knew them in real life…but there were freaks in the world. After all, she was headed there to investigate the murder of this woman's friend.

Jane drummed her fingers on her steering wheel. This woman had brought Michelle White to the party. Someone had been standing near enough to White to stab her without making her question why the person was standing so close. Sasha Henry wasn't just a source. She was a murder suspect.

Jane made a fist and hit the door lock button again. "Get in."

Jake slid across the hood of the car, popped open the passenger door, and climbed in. "Well, what are you waiting for?"

CHAPTER 6

ACCORDING TO THE RADIO, there was a crash on the Terwilliger curves, which meant the hour she had given herself to get across town was just enough.

"Sorry I let the side down," Jake said.

"Excuse me?"

"My curse. Traffic-stopping curves."

"Huh?" Jane's eyes were trained on the cars ahead of her, and her mind on the questions she wanted to ask Sasha.

"Jacob *Terwilliger* Crawford?"

"Your middle name is Terwilliger? Like Sideshow Bob?"

"And the deadly curves on the highway."

"Family name, I assume?"

"But of course."

Jane inched her way into the lane she needed. She had Jake all to herself for an hour, at least. Now was as good a time as any to address the Gemma situation. Her heart pounded. She hated to do it, but if he couldn't tell what he was doing to poor Gemma, he had to be told. "So, about Gemma."

"Good kid."

"Yeah, she's twenty-five. I don't think she thinks of herself as a kid."

"Right-oh."

"Be serious for a second." Jane licked her lips. This was hard. "You're around too much. You're making her think you're into her. It's not fair."

"I can't help other people's misconceptions."

"Yes, you can."

"I don't give her any reason to think I like her. In fact, she's an idiot if she thinks I do. First of all, she's too old. She's like, what? A solid three years older than me? A cougar. Not my thing."

Jane exhaled slowly through tight lips, a thing she was doing a lot of lately. "Be serious. She's gorgeous, smart, and completely infatuated with you. You're going to end up hurting her, and then things will be awkward. You need to start hanging out with your other friends more."

"What other friends?" Jake rolled his eyes.

"Voted most popular at Prez Prep senior year, and you ask what other friends?"

"Dark ages, Jane."

"Your friends from uni, then. I don't care who. You need to go find your other friends."

"Are you trying to get rid of me?"

She was tempted to say yes, but in reality it was the last thing she wanted. She dismissed reality for the moment. "I'm trying to protect Gemma's feelings."

"If you want to get rid of me, just say so. If I'm a pain, if you don't like me around, say the word and I'm gone."

"You *are* a pain."

Jake popped the door open. He leaned out of the car. "Adios."

"See?" They were crawling at five miles an hour, but Jane braked hard.

Jake jerked forward. Then he sat back and shut the door. "My old friends…" He sighed. "It's not the same anymore."

"Since you lost your parents?"

"Yes and no. I mean yes, because that made me take a good, long look at life, and I saw that it sucked, and I hated it."

"And your friends were included in that list?"

"No. But I hit the road. I spent a year in Thailand doing great things. When I came home…" He shook his head. "What can you expect? I don't really want to go get blotto at Bubbles watching girls dance, after spending a year saving girls from sex trafficking."

"That's not what your old friends do."

"Wanna bet? Take the next exit. I'll show you where my old friends spend Friday nights."

"Then make new friends."

"I did." He tilted his head and gave her a cheesy grin.

"Make more new friends. Cut your random visits down to one a week or less. Spend time with men or something."

Jake crossed his arms behind his head. "As you wish."

"Oh, shut up."

Jake looked far more at ease at the Henry house than Jane felt. The place had the gravitas of a palace, propped on the side of the hill as it was, overlooking downtown Portland—from the west.

"Don't stare," Jake whispered.

Jane pulled her eyes down from the coffered ceiling of the foyer. A maid had opened the door and let them in. The Henrys had live-in uniformed help. She had *been* live-in help for a short while, the year before. Jake's live-in help. She trained her eyes on the wall.

A woman with bobbed silver hair, wearing dark jeans with light stitches and a cashmere sweater, padded into the foyer. "Welcome." She held her hand out to Jane. "Why don't you come with me into the living room?"

The living room was smaller than Jane expected, but still very formal. She was thankful it wasn't her job to keep the stains off of the white rugs and the linen-covered furniture. "Thank you so much for letting us stop in."

"Of course." Sasha waved towards the sofa.

Sasha perched on the edge of an armchair.

Jane ran through her list of questions, trying to land on the one that would help make Sasha comfortable, but still get her the right information, right away.

"I am so sorry that my fundraising event had such a terrible cost for you." Jake leaned forward, his face a picture of concern.

Jane watched him closely. His eyes were moist and his face flushed. He looked completely sincere.

"Thank you." Sasha pressed her lips together and closed her eyes. She took a deep breath, then opened her eyes again. "You're Bob and Pam Crawford's boy, aren't you?"

"Yes, ma'am." He nodded.

"Well then, you certainly understand the struggles ahead." She returned Jake's look of sympathy with one of motherly concern.

"I do."

"Are any of Michelle's family in the area?" Jane asked. She was grateful that Jake had joined her. He was a steadfast friend, for sure, but she didn't want him to run away with the conversation. She'd never learn to do this if she relied on him for everything.

Sasha shook her head. "No. When she retired, she moved to Nevada to live nearer her son and his family."

"What brought her to Portland?"

"She had some work to take care of." Sasha dabbed at her eyes with a handkerchief. "I'm sorry, I just can't believe she's gone."

"I understand." Jake's voice was low, and a little husky.

"She had retired though, generally speaking?"

"Yes, she had. Lucky thing. I wanted to retire at fifty-five too, but it's not happening."

"What did she do before she retired?" Jane tried to match Jake's naturally sympathetic tone, but her nerves made her voice shake. She did care about this woman who had lost her friend, but she was still scared to death of being recognized as a fraud.

"Do you know Trillium Montessori? That was her baby."

"No…I'm sorry, I don't." Jane kicked herself for not having a notepad on hand. And yet, taking notes could ruin the mood.

"It's a preschool and kindergarten in Lake Oswego. She founded it about twenty years ago. My kids went there. That's how I met her." Sasha's voice broke. Her eyes were red and her cheeks were stained with fresh tears.

She wasn't truly ready to talk yet.

"Did she come back to town to check on the new administrator?" Jake asked.

"No, she came to finalize some things about the sale. The sale of the school was what enabled her to retire early." A light buzzing noise caught Sasha's attention. She picked a phone off of the antique side table and checked the screen. "I'm sorry, this is Michelle's daughter-in-law. I need to take the call." She answered the phone, then stood up.

Jake followed her lead.

Jane considered the sale of the school. Could something have gone wrong with it? She'd have to find out who the buyer was, for sure.

Jake took hold of her elbow gently and prodded her to get up.

Sasha stood by the living room door, talking on her phone, but looking towards the foyer, eyebrows lifted.

They left, nodding their goodbyes.

The drive home was just as slow, since their conversation with Sasha had been cut short.

Jake reclined his seat and closed his eyes.

"My next step is to find out who bought Trillium Montessori." Jane thought about telling Jake to take notes while she drove.

Jake yawned.

"Then I need to figure out if anyone the buyer knew happened to be at the party. As well as what might have possibly gone wrong with the sale." Jane switched lanes. "And I need to find out if any of the guests had had kids at Trillium. They could tell me a lot about Michelle, I bet." She needed to get over one more lane so she wouldn't miss her exit, but the traffic was bumper to bumper and no one would let her through. She tried to pay equal attention to the cars in front of her and the ones to her side, but it felt like being in a pinball machine. Fear that she was going to kill them both tied for top place with fear that she would screw up the investigation. One of the two was going to give her a heart attack.

Jake didn't answer.

"Do you have the guest list?" Jane tried to nose into the next lane, but the driver next to her laid on his horn. Jane wrenched the wheel and almost overshot.

"Just take the highway the whole way." Jake turned on the radio. "Smooth jazz, Jane, really?" He clicked it over to the Fish.

"What about the guest list?"

He mouthed along with the song.

"Are you ignoring me now?" Jane gritted her teeth. He was…a pain.

"I think I used up my quota of friend time for the week."

"Fine." Jane didn't need him to get the answers to her questions, but she did have to drive him back to her apartment since that's where his car was.

They rode in silence, Jane brainstorming new questions, but in her head, and Jake pretending to care about the top ten Christian songs of the week.

Back at her apartment, she walked him to his car. "Thanks, Jake. You were right about coming with me."

Jake looked past her, toward her apartment window. "And you're right about Gemma." He popped open his car door. "But *you* are going to miss me."

He kissed the top of her head, climbed into his car, and drove away.

She had hardly had time to miss her ex-almost-fiancé, so she doubted she'd be overwhelmed with grief because Jake cut his impromptu visits down to once a week.

CHAPTER 7

"HOW DID IT GO?" Gemma handed Jane a cup of tea as soon as she stepped into the apartment.

"Pretty well. I think I have some idea of where to start, at least." Jane settled into the corner of the sofa. She set her teacup on the coffee table and rested a notebook on her knee.

"Isaac called while you were out."

Jane closed her eyes and counted to ten.

"I'm worried about you, Jane. You don't seem to be grieving this loss at all, even though he was a big part of your life."

Jane rocked her head back and forth, trying to loosen her tense shoulders. "I should be crying more. I'm sure I should, but it's not happening."

"That's what I was thinking. When Nick and I broke up, I cried for weeks."

"But you found out he cheated on you, right? I mean, he had to marry the girl. I think I would cry for weeks if I had found out that Isaac had done that." Jane exchanged her notepad for her teacup. "But I dumped Isaac. Maybe girls don't cry when they end the relationship."

"I don't know…"

"Maybe I didn't really love him." Jane sipped her tea. "I know we dated a long time by some standards, but he's been gone for almost six months straight. In *Robin Hood,* Lady Cluck said, 'Absence makes the heart grow fonder,' but it didn't."

"You're quoting a cartoon chicken?"

Jane shrugged. "Why not, if she's right? I was really infatuated with Isaac…but I'm afraid I didn't really love him."

"But wasn't it love at first sight?" Gemma sat down at Jane's feet.

Jane pictured Isaac the first day she met him at school. Tall, adorable, smart. "Infatuation at first sight, anyway."

"But you were star-crossed, doesn't that count for anything?"

"We were Bible-school-administration-crossed. It's not exactly the same thing." All of a sudden, Jane's heart hurt. It was like a sharp pang, like someone squeezed it tight. Isaac was so smart, and funny, and handsome, and nice. Her eyes stung with tears. She rested her chin on her knees and tried not to cry.

"Tell me again why you dumped him, because I just don't get it."

Jane wiped her eyes. She pictured them on the hood of his car watching the city of Portland sparkle in the distance. "He…he didn't respect me."

"Are you sure? Because I thought he really, really loved you."

"No. I don't think he did. He didn't—" A sob broke out despite her best effort to stifle it. "He didn't…" She took a deep breath. "I'm sorry." She laid her head on her folded arms and cried. The tears were hot and salty and felt as good rolling down her face as the pain in her heart felt awful.

"Don't be sorry. I think you are finally starting to deal with your loss."

She wiped her eyes. "He treated me like I was an accessory. A thing to make his life complete instead of a person who had her own call from God."

"The missionary thing?"

"Umm hmm." Jane dabbed her nose with a paper napkin.

"Please don't be mad at me, but you dumped him because he didn't respect your call to missions…and yet you aren't, like, trying to be a missionary."

"I can't explain it, Gemma, which is probably part of why Isaac couldn't respect it. I know in my heart God wants to use me overseas, but the only directions I have right now are to 'wait.' God didn't say, 'Go to Montreal with Isaac.'" Jane tried to sip her tea, but it burned the tip of her tongue.

"What did God say about Montreal?"

"He was kind of silent about it. Like I was supposed to use the brains he gave me to make that decision. And listening to the way Isaac talked about his work and my call and stuff…I don't think that I could follow God's best plan for me *and* marry Isaac. I wanted to, though. I really, really wanted to." Jane squeezed her eyes shut.

Gemma leaned her head against Jane's knee. "I know you did." Her voice was a quiet hush.

***

By midnight Jane had a flow chart of case notes that was four pages long.

Michelle's backstory inspired any number of questions that needed answers, as did her Google search.

The internet news seemed to love a Christmas charity killing. The protesters were a particularly popular feature online. A heated discussion had risen up on an anti-gun forum. Since the weapon of choice this time had been a knife, the pro-gun people had flooded the site. The initial posts were mostly neener-neener pro-gun posts, but it eventually evolved into a deep discussion of the facts of the case, most of which were new to Jane.

One poster, who went by "Bang-Bang Bambi's Dead," caught Jane's eye right away. From Bang-Bang's posts Jane learned that the HLP protesters had been targeting local dairies for the last twelve months. Jane couldn't recall seeing any of that in the news, but it didn't surprise her. Known for their nonviolent protests against food they deemed unhealthy, which usually included animal products and anything highly processed, the Human Liberation Party had taken a stand against pasteurization.

Against pasteurization?

Jane googled that as well. Pasteurization killed germs that killed people, but pasteurization also killed bacteria that promoted healthful digestion. If she had to pick a side, offhand and just from what she saw at a glance, she would have to go pro-pasteurization. But then, she drew a picture of a barn next to her notes…on the whole, she didn't trust people enough to buy raw milk and cream from just anyone. And at the same time, she'd seen enough exposé news about how animals get treated in huge farm corporations that she didn't think mechanization made things better.

Not that she trusted the news much either.

She scratched out her barn picture.

Mistrust was a handier quality for a detective than for a missionary. So, she'd have to use it now, but work on improving her ability to trust people in the future.

Did she trust Bang-Bang's posts? That was a good question, since Bang-Bang was also the only person in the conversation who mentioned that Michelle Smith had been an active member of the HLP from 2004 to 2010.

If she did trust Bang-Bang's info, it would mean Michelle's killer might have been targeting the Helpers.

Jane stretched to pop her back. She didn't like where this train of thought was leading.

Who at a charity fundraiser had the most to lose from the protesters?

Helping Hands Early Education Center, represented by her cousin.

Yo-Heaven, represented by Jake.

The dairy industry…

The guest list, if she could ever prize it from her cousin and Jake, could help her find out if anyone at the party had links to the local dairies.

And anyone else HLP had targeted for protest recently. Which included Jake.

She crossed Jake off the list anyway. He was clearly big into God now, and that alone made him not a killer. But also, the "Fro-Yo Murder" wasn't the kind of advertising a business owner wanted at the holidays. There was no way that the killing could help him.

She crossed Gemma off the list too because obviously her cousin didn't kill the guest.

CHAPTER 8

JANE RAN THE SWEEPER through the sanctuary at Columbia River Christian Church. The old brush sweeper was quieter than a vacuum, so the elders preferred it be used in this room. She kind of liked the idea, but it wasn't the most efficient way to get the pine needles out of the carpet. And taking down the month-old pine boughs and wreaths made a big mess.

Real tree branches smelled like Christmas, and Christmas Eve service at Columbia River CC with Isaac by her side had been one of the nicest Christmas Eve services she'd ever attended. But now that she had dumped Isaac, she sort of thought she ought to dump his church, too.

She didn't want to break up with Columbia River. It was a good church. Solid teaching, close small groups, friendly staff. Specially selected and fully funded missionaries who would get to spend their furloughs recuperating instead of fundraising.

She lifted the sweeper up to the first step of the stage and ran it the length. It was the Daniels' family church. Last year, when she and Isaac started dating—but before he left for his summer in Costa Rica—she had made the switch to his church.

Her parents had moved to Phoenix a few years ago, leaving her to define her life in Portland her own way. Why not be a part of the church of the man you wanted to marry?

And, she thumped her sweeper up another step, this is why.

If she had stayed at her own church, she wouldn't have to leave it now.

"Can you pass me that candle?" A woman Jane had recently met, named Gail, reached down to Jane.

Jane picked up a midnight-blue taper and passed it to Gail.

"Thanks, kiddo."

Jane nodded with a smile, but didn't say anything. She plopped her sweeper down on the stage. When she was done with the sanctuary, she had to move into the multipurpose event room. Tearing down Christmas was a big job.

"So Jane," Gail called from the ladder. "Is Isaac still home?"

Jane nodded. Her eyes filled with tears. She chewed on her bottom lip. Letting herself cry about it last night had maybe been a bad idea, if it meant his name was going to turn on the waterworks from now on.

"Are you guys coming to the watch night party?"

Jane shook her head no. She couldn't trust herself to speak.

Gail climbed off the ladder. "Hey, are you okay?" She frowned with concern.

Jane nodded, but it was a lie. Tears spilled down her cheeks.

Gail took her arm and led her out of the sanctuary. "You need a break."

Gail took her to the fireside room and clicked on the gas fireplace. "Sit." She sat on the hearth and patted a cushion next to her. "All is not well in paradise."

Jane wiped her eyes. "No, it's not."

"What did he do?"

Jane smiled through her tears. "Why do you think it was him?"

"I watched him grow up. I know he can be a bit difficult."

"Yeah..." Was difficult the word she would pick? He didn't argue or fight. He wasn't a yeller or anything like that. No temper at all, to speak of. But...yeah. He was difficult. "We just...we want different things from life."

"Ahh." Gail patted Jane's knee. "The course of young love never did run smooth."

"No, I guess not."

"So how are you guys going to resolve your troubles?"

Jane shrugged.

"Oh." Gail's voice fell. "I am very fond of Isaac. But...he's not an easy kid. I was really happy he had found you."

"He's a wonderful person." Jane sniffled. He was wonderful, kind of. Just...bossy. And dismissive.

"Yeah, but you're thinking he's not the wonderful person for you?"

Jane nodded. "I should probably finish my work."

"You've got time. Tell me everything."

Jane bit her tongue. It was tempting to get everything off her chest, but she didn't really know Gail, and what was there that needed to be said? She shrugged again. "We really like each other, but we aren't going the same direction in life. And liking each other isn't always enough."

"Do you love each other?"

"What's love but friendship with a ton of infatuation attached? Of course we were in love. Or at least something like that."

"He was gone an awful lot this last year." Gail patted Jane's back.

"Yeah."

"So you've hardly had any time to spend together."

"And he wants to jump straight from that to me moving away."

"Did he propose?"

Jane nodded again. She was probably saying too much.

"But you didn't accept."

"How could I? I have to follow God's call, not Isaac's."

"You were infatuated with each other, but..." Gail paused. She looked over Jane's shoulder and shook her head like she was sending someone away.

Jane wanted to see who was back there, but she kept her face forward.

"You were infatuated with each other, but when push came to shove, it just wasn't enough."

"I guess not."

"It happens, Jane. Even with really great guys who you admire and find attractive."

"We just met at the wrong time. Maybe if we were older..."

"But you fear that if you were older, you probably wouldn't have ever met."

"Exactly." Jane sat up a little. "That's exactly right. It seems like your future husband should be someone you could have met at any point in your life, because God was planning on doing the same work with you both."

"It's okay to have dated someone even if it didn't work out. You're young still."

"I'm not even done with school yet."

"Exactly." Gail gave Jane a side hug. "Kiddo, heartbreak is hard, even if you feel like you picked it yourself. Most of us have been there."

Another tear escaped. Jane took a deep breath. "I think I need to work before I drown in my own tears."

"Good idea. There's a time for everything. A time to weep and a time to sweep."

Jane laughed. "And right now it's time to sweep."

Gail walked to the door. "I've got tree branches to recycle and candles to switch out, but find me before you leave if you want to talk some more, okay? And, you know, today it feels like heartbreak. Next time you and Isaac talk, it might feel like something else altogether."

It would be very hard to leave Columbia River. Everyone, absolutely everyone she had met, was exactly as amazing as Gail.

This cleaning day would have to be her absolute last stop at this church. If she let herself come back to one more small group, or one more service, she'd never be able to walk away.

And if she stayed here…she might change her mind about Isaac again.

On her drive home, Jane tuned into the local news. The Fro-Yo Murder led the news break. The Crawford Family Restaurant Corporation was paying the funeral expenses for the Smith family. A good deed—but also a smart business move on Jake's part. The city liked to see big companies take care of small people.

The funeral reminded Jane that she wanted to try and meet Michelle's family. If her son and his wife had only recently moved away, they might know a lot about who would target Michelle like this.

The funeral might not be the most appropriate place to meet them, but it was the best she could think of, since Michelle's son and his family, according to the news, were only coming to town for the sake of the funeral.

Which led to the next question: why wasn't the family bringing Michelle's body to Nevada for the funeral instead?

She'd have to watch the funeral notices in the newspaper to find out when and where she needed to be. The news made it sound like it would be soon.

She wanted to go over the party guest list before she went to the funeral, so she could compare it with the guest book. Any overlap would be telling. Gemma was probably home, and yet…she remembered what Jake had said the night of the crime. Gemma had an official guest list, but he had called in favors to fill the party out.

She headed to Maywood, the little suburban city just outside of town where the Crawford family restaurant business had its main offices. Most likely Jake would be in his office working midday on Thursday. They could shut the door of his office and have a nice long chat about that guest list of his.

Jane climbed the stairs to the offices on top of the second-to-last Roly Burger restaurant. She knocked and then let herself in. She had a twinge of fear, but Marjory, Jake's intimidating aunt, was not at the desk.

The girl at the desk was much younger than Marjory.

And very cute.

Jane sniffed. Curly blonde hair. Freckles. An upturned nose? Really? Jane wondered if the girl could type, but then noticed that the girl *was* typing—and talking on the phone at the same time—both at lightning speed. The girl looked up for a second and nodded towards a row of chairs against the wall.

Jane almost sat, but reminded herself that she was a private detective, not the maid, this time.

She ignored the receptionist and pushed open Jake's office door.

Before she could say hello, a man in the chair opposite Jake stood up, pushing his chair into Jane's knees. "I think you're going to regret this, Crawford."

Jake's face was brilliant red. His shoulders were up to his ears, and a vein on his neck was throbbing. "And I think you are overreacting. When you are ready to talk man-to-man, I'll be here."

Jane scooted to the wall next to the door. Jake's eyes were glued to the angry man, and he didn't acknowledge her.

The angry man snarled—or at least that was the best word Jane could come up with. It was a businesslike kind of snarl. Very television drama. He pushed his way out the door, stomping so loudly they could still hear him on the stairs.

"Jane." Jake stared out the door. "That was the mayor of Maywood, and he wants junk food blue laws in our gentle little town."

"He's not a Helper, is he?"

"Not that he admits to." Jake took a seat—on top of his desk. "You, however, are a sight for sore eyes. What can I do for you?"

Jane rolled her eyes. "I want the guest list to the fundraiser. Not the official one though, the augmented one. The one you filled out that has pretty much everyone on it."

Jake furrowed his brow. "I could do that for you."

"But?"

"But you'd have to do something for me in return."

"Of course I would." Jane sat down in the chair the angry mayor had so violently vacated.

"Move to Maywood."

"Excuse me?"

"Move to this cute little suburban mini-town so you can vote against the blue laws, and so I can come see you as often as I want without giving your cousin the wrong idea."

Jane laughed. "Don't be a dope, Jake. I can't abandon Gemma. She can hardly afford half the rent on the apartment, much less the whole thing."

"And whose fault is that? Not yours. Certainly not mine. Why should I have to suffer?"

"Okay, enough of that. Can I have the list?"

"Sure." Jake made a show of digging his phone out of his desk. He frowned, rubbed his forehead, and typed on the touch screen for a few minutes. "Done. I just sent you the list of people I invited via text, and the folks who RSVP'd. I also sent my own notes on who I saw at the party who hadn't let me know they were coming."

"Wow. Really? You had time to take those notes?"

Jake shrugged. "I've got to make the time. Money doesn't make itself. I've already sent thank-you cards to everyone who was there. Ah!" He banged on his phone a bit more. "There you go. That's the address list I sent the thank you's too. It wasn't anything big this year, just a personally signed card and a book of gift certificates. And yes, I have to keep tabs on all of that. It's tax deductible—I hope."

"I'm impressed."

"I wasn't just voted most popular, back in high school. I was also president of Young Entrepreneurs."

"You were?"

He raised his eyebrow. "You don't remember?"

Jane shook her head. She wasn't entirely sure there had been a Young Entrepreneurs at Presbyterian Prep, but apparently his dad had trained him well for his future running the family business. "Remind me: where did you go to college?"

"College? Did I go there?" Jake hopped off of his desk and moved to the window. He stared across Main Street. "Can you believe they want to shut down every business that sells junk food every Sunday? It's preposterous. After-church lunch sales are big money to me."

"You went to college."

"Are you suddenly an education snob, Jane? Is this the Daniels' influence rubbing off on you?"

Jane's face went up twenty degrees. "Never mind. Thanks for the help."

"I entered OSU with two years' college credit under my belt and finished my business degree at nineteen and a half. I went back for an MBA that I took mostly online. Not that I didn't do my fair share of partying anyway, but, yeah. You don't make lifelong college friends when you are in and out like that." Jake drummed his fingers on the window. "But you have to guess which O and which U. Am I a Beaver or a Buckeye? Or maybe Cowboy? You can't make me tell."

"Wow. You're smarter than I thought you were." Jane chewed her bottom lip.

Jake stared out the window, the weight of the world, seemingly, on his shoulders. His forehead was creased in thought, and he looked much older than he had two years ago, when she was sleeping in the maid's quarters at his house. He looked tired. But he was smart, and educated, and had some solid experience under his belt, if he had worked side by side with his dad for the couple of years after he finished school, but before Bob had died…

"Thanks again." Jane turned to leave, not wanting to waste any more of his time.

Jake caught her by the elbow as she turned to go. He leaned close and whispered in her ear, "Don't underestimate yourself, Jane Adler." He brushed her ear with his lips, like a kiss, almost, maybe, and then let her leave.

CHAPTER 9

JANE HUNKERED DOWN over her table at Starbucks. She was making a master list of the notes Jake had sent. She had a feeling the people who hadn't responded to Jake's email, but had come to the party anyway, were the ones to keep her eye out for. She lined out a theory and considered it: Someone knew about the party, and knew that Sasha Henry had invited Michelle Smith. That someone would have had to know enough about the event to know where to go and when, hence the idea that they had an invitation. If they had gone with the express intent to kill, they would not want it known that they were there…so…no RSVP.

Was that too simple?

She wouldn't know until she tested it.

And the funeral would be a decent way to test it…if the person was well enough known by Sasha Henry to know that Sasha was bringing Michelle, he or she would need to be at the funeral for the sake of good appearances. And, if they wanted it known that they were at the funeral, grieving, they would definitely sign the guest book. So someone on Jake's list of people he noticed at the party and had invited, but didn't RSVP, who also happened to sign the guest book, would be someone to look into for motives.

Jane smacked her head. What a convoluted idea. That might possibly be the slowest way ever to find out who might have had a motive.

And yet, it was all she had so far.

Unless of course the killing was related to Michelle's supposed time with HLP. Jane would have to uncover Bang-Bang Bambi's Dead's real identity if she wanted to know how seriously to take that bit of information.

She drummed her fingers on the table. Jake was smart, could he help with cyber spying? She sucked in a breath. He was networking smart—business-savvy smart. She didn't see any signs he could hack it as a hacker.

She scrolled through the contacts on her phone. She was a college-educated (well, almost) twenty-something. Surely she knew someone who could do a little cyber spying.

Ben!

His name on her contact list was a happy surprise. Gemma's stepbrother. He was a tech guy. Designed websites and stuff. He even worked for that Realtor for a while…the one she had met that time the dryer caught fire.

Ben would know how to find out who Bang-Bang was. She texted him a begging message.

While Ben could be of some help, there was one person who would know if Michelle Smith had been an HLP protester.

Rose of Sharon Willis.

She googled Rose of Sharon Willis and HLP. First hit: an HLP Facebook page.

Jane snickered. Of course it would be Facebook. HLP was kind of old-fashioned like that. She "liked" the page and then sent a private message asking Rose of Sharon if she had time to get together. She suggested Sprouted Quinoa, a little vegan raw-food café not far from her apartment. Surely Rose of Sharon wouldn't turn down free raw vegan food.

She sipped her coffee. Her fingers twitched and her heart was racing. She was both overcaffeinated and anxious. She had hit the waiting-game part—would her contacts come through for her? Maybe, maybe not. But if she wanted to solve the murder (and keep her heartache at bay), she had to keep moving.

She had one more obvious move she could make while waiting to hear back from Ben and Rose of Sharon. The event center might well have security footage of the event. As a private detective (in training), it behooved her to ask if she could view it, so, coffee cup in shaking hand, she headed to the Shonley Center.

The event center was an echoey concrete building with high ceilings, faded carpet, and many long halls. It had been built long before she was born—like the 1980s or something—and was showing its age. The dusty smell of an old heating system reminded Jane of the basement of her Bible school. She hummed along to the Peanuts Christmas song while she looked for the security office.

A couple of the many, many spaces were in use. A guy about her age in black khaki pants and a white polo shirt rolled a dolly full of folded tables into a room by the front door. She followed him.

"Hey!" She waved her hand as she called out.

He looked her up and down, and then grinned. "Yeah?"

"Is there, like, an office around here?" Her voice had instantly gone valley girl on her, and she wanted to bite her tongue off. Instead, she flipped her hair over her shoulder and hated herself a little more. She wasn't trying to look like an idiot, but she was sure managing to like a pro.

"Like a business office?" The guy frowned.

'"Yeah, like that." She smiled and tilted her head. She straightened it up with a jerk. She would swear off coffee forever if she couldn't pull herself together.

"I dunno." He leaned on the handle of his dolly. "I'm just here to set up for the model railroad convention. But I'm off in half an hour." He lifted his eyebrows and gave a kind of bro nod.

"Bummer." She shrugged and left.

While this convention facility wasn't the great big one with the pointy towers, it was still big enough that Jane was lost within minutes.

Jane was about to give up and take the first exit she could find, when she ran into an older man wearing a vacuum backpack and headphones.

She got as close as she could and tapped his shoulder.

He shut off his vacuum. "Can I help you?" He had a kind smile and a bushy mustache.

Jane smiled and wrung her hands. The obnoxious valley girl seemed to have been replaced by a simpering child. She tried to pull herself together again. Square her shoulders and all that. Detective. She was a professional detective. "Yes, thank you." She was still grinning, but at least she wasn't rubbing the toe of one shoe with the other. She had both feet firmly on the ground like an adult. "I'm looking for the security office."

The man nodded towards the elevator. "Gotta git yourself upstairs, and then take a left. Then go a long ways. All the way around almost. But if you just keep following the hall, you'll get there." He went back to vacuuming before Jane could ask him if anyone would be there.

But she followed his directions.

The hall was long, and quiet, and spooky. The main overhead lights were off, so the hall was lit with low, energy-efficient lights recessed into the ceilings above each door.

She shivered.

She was glad she had mace clipped to her keychain.

The hall felt like a marathon, her heart raced so hard, but eventually she had made it around the corner to a large double door marked "Security." She knocked, and then opened it up.

"Hi." A girl who looked about Jane's age, but was quite a bit taller and wore a crisp security uniform, smiled at Jane. She was alone in the office. "Can I help you?"

The office was a brightly lit, modern space. Long, clean counters flanked on three sides by walls covered in flat-screen televisions, each one zoomed at a different setting. Almost every screen showed an eerily silent room, but the effect was still dizzying.

Jane sat down.

"I'm Jane. I'm a private detective working on the Fro-Yo Murder case on behalf of the folks who threw the fundraiser."

"Oh, okay. I'm Beth." The security girl rolled her chair around to face Jane. "The police have already seen all the footage we have of the event. Have you talked to them about it yet?" Her face seemed open and friendly, but something about the question made Jane think she would have to prove herself to security.

Jane sat up a little straighter. "No, I wanted to go for firsthand sources before I got the police's opinion on the facts."

"Sure. Okay. I can't show you the footage though. The police had a warrant for it."

Jane nodded. “I understand.” She chewed the inside of her cheek. So many things she would have known if this murder had taken place at the end of next semester instead of now. “So, were you on that night?”

“Nope, but Del, my boyfriend, was.” Beth had a promising twinkle in her eye.

Jane leaned forward and lowered her voice. “Did he see anything suspicious?”

“Well…” Beth eyed the wall of screens before turning back to Jane. “There was this weird kind of shadowy figure in the corner of the room. It looked like someone dressed in dark clothes and leaving quickly, right after the woman screamed.”

“Did he show you the footage?”

“Of course. We all saw it. We have to keep our eye out for anyone we saw in the video returning to the center. Of course, we are really looking for that shadowy figure who left, but between you and me, I don’t know how we’d recognize the person again.”

Jane scanned the wall of televisions. “How many cameras are in that room?”

“Just the one. It’s center on the wall with no exit and has a panoramic of the room.”

“And you all had to watch all of that footage, right?”

“Yup. We did. We watched it several times. In particular, we were looking to see if we could spot the shady-looking character near the victim, and maybe also coming toward the victim."

"You know, I was there that night, and though it was crowded, it didn't seem overwhelming."

"It was pretty mellow at the beginning of the video, but as soon as the protesters came inside, it got a little crazy. From the camera's POV, it was like a room full of little mobs. Gestures got bigger, voices got louder, large groups sort of formed out of the couples and individuals. It was a lot harder to sort through than I expected."

"But did you see more of this shady figure?"

"I didn't."

Jane watched Beth's face. She looked like she had more to say. "Did you see anything suspicious?"

"Yeah, see, this figure kind of steps out from behind someone like a shadow." Beth pointed at one of the televisions. "So the room is mostly dark now, but can you see how the angle is funny? We couldn't really see full bodies of anyone, and even faces were hard to spot, since people were moving around. So everything looked tense, but not strange, and then this person in dark clothes with a dark scarf on, or maybe a wig, kind of steps from crowd to crowd and then leaves. But it went really fast. I almost think she ducked, threw something over her head, and snuck out."

"So you are thinking a girl?"

"It was hard to tell height or anything, but the person seemed smaller, and the scarf was feminine."

"So a girl, or a man with a slight build disguised as a woman." Jane drummed her fingers on the arm of her chair. "If it was a man in a dark sweater or something, and he threw a wig or a scarf over his head, we would all think he was a woman. I sure wish I could see it."

Beth shook her head. "Sorry. I'm not supposed to show this stuff to just anyone."

Jane stood up. "Can I come by again sometime if I think of anything else to ask? Or take you out for coffee?"

"Sure." Beth walked Jane to the door. "I don't mind talking to you about it all, but I don't want to risk my job or anything." She handed Jane a card. "So call and we can get together."

"Thanks so much. I appreciate it."

"I'd walk you out, but I'm not allowed to leave until my partner gets back from the bathroom. But hey, I'll walkie Del and he can walk you out. It's a little creepy around here these days."

"Ah, thank you." Jane headed down the long, too-quiet hallway with one eye out for Del.

CHAPTER 10

DEL MET HER AT THE ELEVATOR. He was kind of a small guy himself, but since he was stuck in the TV room the night of the event, he probably wasn't the mystery killer. Jane noted his slight build and dark hair. Surely, if it had been Del in the video, Beth would have recognized him. But…what if? She smiled, a nervous flutter dancing in her stomach. What if he had slipped out of his office and stabbed Michelle?

Del held the door of the elevator and motioned for Jane to get in. She didn't know where the stairs were…and she wasn't sure that a dark, far-off staircase with a potential killer was a better idea than the elevator.

"Get in." Del's voice was quiet but rough. He frowned.

"Uh…" Jane looked over her shoulder. Maybe she could get Beth to change her mind.

"Get. In." Del had something that might have been a Taser strapped to his Batman-like security-guy utility belt.

Beth may have sent her boyfriend to calm Jane's nerves, but it hadn't worked.

Del let the elevator doors shut. "Stairs it is, then." He stuck his hands in his pockets and ambled off down the hall.

Jane hurried to keep up. Now that he was less likely to kill her…or whatever it was she was scared of, she wanted to ask him a few questions.

"So the night of the murder…that's a lot of TV's to keep an eye on."

"Sure, but I keep a closer eye on the screens where something is supposed to be happening."

"So if the person had snuck in past another camera, would you have seen them?"

"Probably. When the cleaners come through rooms that are supposed to be empty, I always notice. Peripheral vision is a good thing in a room like that."

"So nothing happened in a room it wasn't supposed to happen in."

"I wouldn't have said that for sure the night of." Del slowed down so Jane could keep up with him. "But we've watched all of the film since then. Every hour on every camera. Nobody came in by themselves through a back door. Everyone seemed to come in like they were supposed to. Then again, there were a few big events, so I couldn't say that someone didn't sneak in with a crowd that didn't know them, you know? It was a big night."

"Beth said that the dark—shadowy, or shady—figure was the only thing that stood out in the video. Would you agree?"

"I'm not sure. It seemed to me that a few of the things happening in the video could have been there to distract from the stabbing. For example, early on there was a young guy shilling sample drinks in a really cheesy circus kind of voice. It seemed over the top, and while he was doing it everyone was looking forward instead of around the room at each other."

Jake. Jane rolled her eyes. "What else did you notice?"

"The protesters came sort of in the middle of the party. They mostly stayed in the hall. But some did squeeze in past the folks blocking their entry."

"They did?" Jane stopped. This was the first she had heard about protesters sneaking in. Had one of the Helpers had a grudge against Michelle? She thought back to the anxious protester…Valerie? Valeria? What if she had been with the killer? Or had been the killer?

"Yeah, about four of them did."

"Did any of them match the description of the shady figure you saw?"

"Nope." They arrived at a broad, well-lit staircase in the middle of the building. Del loped down the steps two at a time.

"So, just in your opinion, do you think the shady figure was more likely to have done it, or the protesters who snuck into the party?"

"Couldn't say." He stopped at the bottom of the stairs and waited for her.

"Of course not. So, on the video, what did the protesters who snuck into the party do?"

"They mingled. And they took sample cups from people and threw them away."

"What?" Jane paused.

"I watched them do it at least six times. They walked up to a group, paused like they were chatting, held out their hands and took cups, and then wandered off and threw them away."

"That's…I don't know…a little passive-aggressive, yes?"

"That's how I saw it."

They walked towards the exit, Jane trying to suss what she had heard, when Del grabbed her arm and pulled her into a bathroom. "Shhh."

Jane stiffened. Her heart thundered against her chest and a cold sweat broke out on her forehead. But Del didn't do anything. He just stood there, one finger to his lips. His eyes were scared.

The bathroom door pushed open slowly. An older woman, about five feet tall, with silver hair in a bun, stepped through. "Del?"

Del worked his jaw back and forth.

The small woman looked him up and down. She had on a navy-blue suit with brass buttons and a pair of patent leather pumps. Her name tag said "Lafayette."

"Hey," Del said.

"What are you doing in uniform? You were put on administrative leave." Her frown was serious. The V between her eyes was deep enough to get lost in.

"Yes, ma'am." He chewed his bottom lip and glanced at Jane.

Lafayette looked at Jane as well. "You can move along now."

"Yes, of course." Jane made each step count as she left, hoping to hear what Del had to say, but the two security personnel were silent until the door swung shut again. She paused, ear to the door. Eavesdropping on this unexpected turn was worth the risk.

"Hand me the baton, Taser, and pepper spray." Lafayette's voice was low and hard to hear through the door. Del was silent.

The floor in the bathroom squeaked, so Jane bolted. She was much nearer the exit door when Del and his boss came out. She turned to watch them head back up the stairs.

She had learned two important things from the visit at least, the most important being that you could wander the halls of the massive convention center without getting caught for only so long. And the second thing was that the security guard in charge of monitoring the cameras the night of the murder both fit the description of the killer (to some small extent) and was put on administrative leave.

Jane would be calling Beth tonight for sure.

"I'm starving." Gemma held her phone out like a notepad. "What do you think…burgers, smoothies, or both?"

"Jake is not your personal food delivery boy." Jane sat in front of a list of her suspects. Del had suddenly jumped to the front of the list. She tried calling Beth but had to leave a message. She needed to know so much about this Del character. Starting with his last name. But where he went to school, who his parents were, and how hard up for money he was were high on the list. A hungry man with few scruples who happened to know a person with a grudge…she penciled stars around his name. Of course, those were just guesses. He could be a really good guy with enough to get by on, and he might not have any connection to Michelle at all.

"Jake's a…friend." She grinned and fell backwards onto the sofa. "Right? A goo-o-od friend." She put her phone to her heart. "I don't think you realize how close he and I have gotten this year."

"Yeah, I guess I don't." She prayed that if Gemma asked for food, he'd say no. He owed it to her—er, to Gemma—to help her see the light. "Okay, so at the event, did you notice the protesters who came inside the party?"

"Yeah, of course I did."

"Did they seem to be acting weird to you?"

"A little aggressive, but not weird. I mean, not weird if by weird you mean doing things that surprised me."

"How would you describe their activities?"

"They spread out, talked to people, took their cups and recycled them. They seemed on a friendly mission to change minds, if you know what I mean."

"Did you tell them about the almond-milk alternative smoothies?"

"No. I admit, I was totally overwhelmed by it all. I really didn't know what to do or say to anyone by that time. Didn't you notice any of this?"

"Uhh…" Jane sighed. "I wasn't there. I was still really overwhelmed from the breakup, you know?"

"Poor thing! I can see why you wouldn't want me and Jake hanging around all the time. You're still so tender! I tell you what. I will make sure that Jakey and I take our fun elsewhere." She dialed her phone. "But can I bring something home for you?"

Jane shook her head. Poor, deluded Gemma.

It was just after six, so Jane hid in her bedroom and phoned Trillium Montessori. There was always a chance someone in administration was still around, and anything was better than listening in on Gemma's call.

They answered on the second ring. "Trillium Montessori, this is Carrie speaking."

"Hi, Carrie. I'm Jane Adler." She took a deep breath. "I'm a private detective, and I'm working for the folks who threw the Helping Hands Early Education Center fundraiser where Michelle Smith was killed. Do you have a moment to answer some questions?"

"A detective?" Carrie's voice registered disbelief.

"Yes." Jane attempted to get a deeper, more mature timber out of her voice. "I just have a few questions for you, if you don't mind."

"I guess."

Jane heard papers rustling in the background. "First, if you don't mind, what's your position at the school?"

"I'm April's assistant."

"And…who is April?"

"Oh, sorry. April Harms bought the school from Michelle. She was the senior teacher here before that. Has been with the school since its third year."

"That's great, thank you. And about the sale…had it gone smoothly?"

"Yup. It was a breeze. Michelle was up to finalize some smaller things having to do with the rights to some of the curriculum we use, that she created. Also she decided not to sell the building, so she and April were going to sign a long-term lease agreement."

"Were both of them on board with that?"

"Yeah. It wasn't any big deal. April couldn't get together enough money to buy the school and the building. The lease was going to be a lease-to-buy, though. Provide Michelle with income for retirement and then a lump sum later."

"You seem to know a lot about this." Jane was taking notes as she went, but it was going fast. She needed to stall Carrie so she could get it all down.

"I sit in on the meetings and take dictation. Stuff like that. But none of it was particularly secret."

"Carrie, would you mind if I came down and saw the school?"

"Why not? We're all closed up right now, but you could come tomorrow morning. Probably best if you come by before nine when our classes start though."

"Thank you so much. That would be perfect." Jane got the address and let Carrie go. If Carrie could be trusted, then April Harms wasn't likely to be the murderer, but it wouldn't hurt to see her in person. Especially since April had known Michelle for so long. She'd probably know more dirt about Michelle than anyone else.

Since there was every chance that Gemma was in the other room pouting—or worse, crying—about Jake not wanting to get together, Jane stayed in her room for the rest of the night.

Tomorrow she had two big houses to clean and one school to visit. Not too bad for a housecleaning detective.

CHAPTER 11

JANE'S PHONE DINGED as she pulled into the Trillium Montessori parking lot. A new email—from PayPal? Jane opened it. Three hundred and fifty dollars from Jake for "expenses" paid through her Good Clean Houses business account. She took a deep breath. What was this new scheme of his? She checked her clock—only eight. She had time to call him before she went inside.

"Jake, what is this?"

"What is what? Do you know how early it is?" Jake yawned.

"Don't pretend you aren't up."

"I'm not up."

"You've been using your computer."

"You are a very good spy."

Jane rolled her eyes. "What expenses are you paying me for?"

"The expenses incurred for solving the murder that occurred at my first-ever fundraiser for educating homeless preschoolers."

"You're paying me for this?"

Jake yawned again. “I know. Crazy, right?”

“Thank you?” Jane wasn’t sure what to think. If she wanted to pursue detection, she needed paying clients. But taking money from Jake just felt wrong. On the other hand, he would be the one most likely to hire her in this situation.

“You’re welcome. And it’s cheaper than bringing you and that cousin of yours lunch and dinner six days a week.” Jake cleared his throat. “Just solve it, okay?”

“Jake…”

“I did not go out with Gemma last night. I called a guy and hung out doing guy things. Are you happy?”

Jane couldn’t hide her laugh. “Yes, I’m happy. The sooner Gemma realizes you’re just not that into her, the better for her.”

“Are you done lecturing me? I’d like to go back to sleep.”

“Yes.” Lecturing? Jane didn’t like the sound of that. She was his buddy, not his mom. “Sorry. And thanks for the expenses. I’ll try and use it wisely.”

“Just remember, whatever you do, work at it with all your heart, working for God and not people, okay? Detecting, schooling, missioning, whatever. Just do your best and make God proud.”

Jane grinned. Sometimes Jake surprised her. “Yes. I will.”

She let him go and contemplated her expense fund. A little money could smooth the path to information. Did people want cash to talk, or coffee? She’d have to read each person as they came, and right now it was time to read Carrie, assistant to April Harms.

The reception desk was in the center of a small, colorful foyer fully decked out for every major winter holiday. "Carrie?" Jane offered her hand to the woman behind the desk.

"Yes, are you Jane?" She shook Jane's hand.

"Yes, thanks so much for letting me stop by."

"Of course." Carrie's thick brown hair hung in a braid that landed at the hem of her wooly sweater. With her skinny figure, makeup-free face, and outfit made from entirely natural fibers, Jane could see Carrie fitting in with Rose of Sharon's Helpers. Maybe it did make sense that Michelle had once been a protester. "What can I show you?" Carrie waved her hand, indicating the hall that led to the classrooms.

"We can just chat, if that's okay. I'm trying to learn a little more about Michelle. I know she has one son, married, living in Nevada. Does she have any other family in town?"

"I don't know. Maybe she does, but I never talked to her about her family."

"What made her decide to sell the school and retire?"

"Her grandkids." Carrie sat down in her rolling office chair. She motioned to a bright green armchair.

Jane took a seat. "Did she seem excited for the change?"

"Yes and no. She was really excited to see her grandkids more and to live someplace warm and dry, but every now and then I'd catch her in a bit of a melancholy mood. But it makes sense, you know? She built this school from nothing." Carrie sighed. "Change is hard, even when it's something you're looking forward to."

"That's true." Jane relaxed back into her seat. "How did the parents take the change?"

"Everyone loves April, so that wasn't a problem at all."

"Everyone?"

"Oh yes, everyone. The PTO, the alumni. She's just a lot of fun, and she's kind of like an extension of Michelle. I don't think it would have worked if Michelle had sold to a stranger."

"Did anyone have a particularly hard time saying goodbye to Michelle?" Jane really wanted to know if anyone was especially happy to see her go, but wanted to work her way up to that question.

"Oh yes! A few of our families have been here for several years. We're just a preschool and kindergarten, but if you are a big family, you could end up here for a decade. And one family, the Chadwicks, they are on their second generation! It's hard to believe it's been long enough, but…they had a lot of kids, and their youngest three went here. Now their oldest kids have kids in the school, if that makes sense. Lots of big families here."

"What's tuition these days?"

"It's eight to twelve thousand a year, depending on what age, but there are family discounts."

Jane swallowed. That was more than her tuition at Presbyterian Preparatory High School had been. “Does she ever run into trouble with families that can’t pay?”

Carrie rolled her eyes. “Yes. It drives me batty, too. Michelle was wonderful about scholarships, grants, and family discounts. There was no need for anyone to get into financial difficulty. I mean, of course, if you don’t have the money, you shouldn’t say you do and enroll in the first place, but if you are a Trillium family and run into hard times…Michelle—and now April—has always been willing to find a way to work with you.”

“Can you think of anyone who might have a grudge against Michelle—for anything at all? Tuition costs? Something that happened at the school? Or even something in her personal life?”

Carrie drew her eyebrows together. “I really didn’t want to have to mention this, but I’d probably better. If the police come in to talk, I’ll have to tell them anyway.”

Jane leaned forward, elbows on her knees.

“The Miters…” She shook her head. “Oh, I hate to even say this. The Miters actually owe us one hundred thousand dollars, and Michelle has been fighting the situation in court for the last three years.”

A thrill went through Jane. “That’s a whole lot of money. How does a family end up owing their preschool that much money?”

“They were another big family. They had four kids in the school for four years...”

“But they would have had to have all of the kids there the whole time without paying...they didn’t do that, did they?”

“No...they had sent six kids through the school altogether. And for each one of them, there would come a time where their checks stopped clearing. They would rack up a debt with us, tuition, fees, and then the bounced-check fees.” Carrie rubbed her eyes in exasperation. “But when fall enrollment came around, they’d enroll whoever was old enough at the time. They’d pay a couple of months’ tuition up front plus some of their back fees. Michelle was always willing to work with them. But then, at the end, when they had the four kids here at once, they just stopped paying.”

“But still, the fees could hardly have reached one hundred thousand, could they?”

“Michelle had to take them to court for the money, once it got over thirty thousand. She just couldn’t pay her bills with that much outstanding. The court decided for us, and included legal fees. Michelle didn’t want them to have to pay that much, she really didn’t.”

“If they couldn’t afford tuition, how were they going to be able to afford the judgment?”

Carrie shook her head. “You got me. Personally, I think hitting them with such a huge amount made it even less likely that they would pay up.”

“I’d have to agree. So what do the Miters look like?”

“Jason is about forty-five, greying hair. He’s kind of tall and skinny. Tammy isn’t much younger, I’d say. She’s cute, a butterball, but all dimples and smiles. Every time she told you she would pay up right away, you just believed her. She’s that type of person.”

“How tall would you say Jason was?”

“Average tall, I guess. What’s that, six feet maybe? He wasn’t short at all, but he wasn’t bumping his head on the door, if you know what I mean.”

“Sure, I get it.” Jane stood up. “I really appreciate the time you gave me.”

“I don’t think the Miters would have killed Michelle. They’re terrible with money, but they’re really nice.”

“Oh, of course! I know what you mean. But the whole conversation was helpful.”

Carrie walked Jane to the parking lot. She looked back at the school for a second, and then repeated her affirmation of the Miter family. “I mean it, they are good people.”

Jane paused. “Would you ever let kids of theirs back in the school?”

“Well, no, but that doesn’t make them killers.”

Jane smiled. Of course it didn't. It just made them suspects. Really, really good suspects.

Beth from the event center security called Jane back shortly after Jane got home. She jumped right into her purpose before Jane could even say hello.

"I'm a bit frazzled, to be perfectly frank. I think you might know why."

"Because Del wasn't supposed to be at work, even though he was there?"

"That would be it. He's on administrative leave—a disciplinary action—I don't even know what he did."

"Why was he pretending to be at work?" Jane perched on the edge of her seat, pen in hand. This call couldn't have come at a better time. She could get all of her Del questions answered and then compare the Del situation with the Miter family. If she was lucky, she wouldn't have to follow up with the questions about Michelle's time with the HLP at all.

"It was a shift we were working together. We had plans for the day. Dumb little things you do when you're dating a coworker. He would bring me coffee, I would page him to the office for a kiss. Just dumb stuff. But if he didn't come, he'd have to tell me why."

"What about the person who was supposed to cover his shift?"

"That's a good question too." Beth sounded exhausted. "That person seems to have colluded with Del on this little scheme, and now he's on admin leave too…guess who has to cover all of their shifts?"

"That would be you." Jane chuckled sympathetically.

"Yup. And I don't have time for it. But I can't turn it down."

"How many of you are there in security?"

"About a dozen," Beth said. "More like ten now, though. And that's hardly enough. You've seen the place. It's huge. And it's open crazy hours."

"What did Del do to get in trouble?"

"He won't tell me, so it's got to be bad. He's acting all heroic about it like he's protecting me, but that's stupid. We've been together seven months now. He can tell me anything."

Seven months. Jane stifled a smirk. Practically married. "What are you going to do now?"

"Work too much, I guess. I don't want to be a jerk to my boyfriend at Christmas, but I need a little space if he's not going to be honest with me."

"Is Del from around here?"

"Sure. He's from Gladstone. He's always lived here."

Gladstone? That little suburb wasn't too far from Trillium Montessori…basically just across the river, if Jane was picturing it right. "How old is he?"

"See, that's the other thing, older guys are supposed to be mature, responsible. Del is thirty-two, but he's acting like he's twelve."

Thirty-two…Jane considered that. He was just, almost, young enough to have been in the first class at Trillium. On the other hand…he was also old enough to have a kid that went there. "Does Del have family in town? Parents, brother or sister? Kids?"

"Yeah, sure. His parents are here. He also has a brother who lives in Seattle. No kids."

No kids… "So what do you think Del did to get in trouble at work?"

Beth sighed. "Honestly? I hate to even say it because it makes me sound like a jealous loser, but I kind of wonder if he had some girl up in the office with him. I mean, what else could it have been that he can't tell me about?"

What else indeed? Maybe sneaking out of the office to kill Michelle Smith. Jane kept the thought to herself, but considered it carefully nonetheless. "Does the security room have a security camera on it? Could you go back and watch the video of it?"

Beth was silent. "Well, now that you mention it, I feel really stupid. There is a camera. We all know it's there. We just don't get to monitor it ourselves. I don't know that it is monitored, actually, or who does it. But probably someone reviewed it, and that's how they know what he was up to. Then again, maybe he only got caught because there was an actual security issue."

"If you could find out more about that camera, you could find out what he had going on that night."

"Man, I'd like to do that." Beth sounded wistful.

"Why don't you?" Jane desperately wanted to be invited to view the film, but tried to keep her hope out of her voice.

"It's not a bad idea. At the least I can ask the boss about it. She might just tell me what he did, anyway."

"Lafayette?"

"Yeah, Meryl Lafayette. She runs the show here. How did you meet her?"

"She sort of caught Del when he was walking me out. She didn't introduce herself or anything, but I saw her name tag."

"I'm going to talk to her. She's bound to tell me something useful, after all, I am filling in some major gaps in her schedule on very short notice." Beth's voice had gotten a little of its oomph back. "Have you talked to her about the night of the murder yet? She probably knows everything the cops do. She's got an in at the force."

"She does?"

"Yeah, one of her kids is a cop. Anyway, I'm actually here for a morning shift. This was supposed to be my day off. I think I can catch Meryl and have a chat with her on my first break."

"Will you call me if you think it had anything at all to do with the murder?"

"Del? Are you kidding?"

Jane tried to laugh a little. "Not Del, per se, just anything that went on that she tells you about."

Beth was quiet for a long moment. "I don't know. It will depend on what I hear."

"I understand. Thanks for calling."

Jane ended the call disappointed. So close to hearing something useful, and then cut off. Del was local, Del could have possibly gone to Trillium as a student, but she hadn't gotten any information about where he went to school or if he had maybe known Michelle's son. She could think of several horrible, nightmarish reasons why someone might want to murder their old preschool teacher, but it seemed as though if Michelle were a child abuser, someone would have hinted at it by now.

No, if Del killed her, it wasn't likely because of something that had happened to him twenty-five years ago.

Jane hated to admit it, but she needed Rose of Sharon, so she could learn something about Michelle's days with HLP. Once she had done that, she would have a fuller picture of Michelle Smith and the people most likely to want her dead.

But first she had to change into her work clothes. Suburban houses didn't clean themselves.

CHAPTER 12

IT HAD BEEN A VERY LONG DAY. Her head was spinning from all of the news she had gathered. And it had been a very long Christmas break. In fact, it had been twelve days since Isaac had come back to town, and three since his last text message—not that she had read any of them. The twelve days of Christmas, in its own really depressing way. Jane threw her phone across the room. It landed with a soft thud in her laundry basket. She rolled over and pressed her face into her pillow so she could cry without being heard, but she couldn't cry.

She rolled over onto her back. She was wrong. Isaac had come home from that stupid university in Canada fourteen days ago. Fourteen miserable, lonely days.

It was December twenty-ninth, and in two days she was going to have to spend New Year's Eve alone.

Ben hadn't replied with any information about Bang-Bang, the internet gun advocate.

Rose of Sharon hadn't responded to her invitation.

Jake hadn't called.

Gemma was moping.

And Jane had cleaned a condo on the seventh floor in a building with a broken elevator.

She pressed her pillow to her face to scream but didn't have the energy.

Someone knocked softly on her door.

"Yes?" It came out like a bark and it felt good.

"I'm lonely." Gemma came in and sat on the floor. "And I'm broke, and I'm hungry. Jake isn't returning my calls, my last client delivered. Come out with me, somewhere, anywhere."

Jane glanced towards her phone. "I should really try and…" She sighed.

"You should really lie around waiting for your phone to ring? God didn't invent cell phones so you could stay at home." Gemma smiled, one eyebrow raised. "Just out for dinner, or something."

"You're broke, so I'm buying?"

"How about we invite ourselves to someone's party?"

Jane shook her head. "I wouldn't even know where to start."

"I've got it. It's okay. There is a little thing going on tonight, and we can go because I was the hostess's sister's doula. I saw it on Twitter."

"A Twitter party?" Jane looked out the window. It was only early evening, but it was dark as night. "A party at six? Is it a five-year-old's birthday?"

"Nope. And it'll be fun. We don't leave for a couple of hours, so we have time to get absolutely adorable." Gemma pulled Jane up by her arm. "Come on now, hair and makeup. No Plain Jane tonight."

Gemma's idea of a party and Jane's were different, though Jane had to admit she hadn't been to a real party since high school. Since then, she had sort of limited herself to church college group events…retreats, hikes, wholesome activities like that. This thing, however, was a real party.

The old Portland house off of Hawthorne was strung with colored Christmas lights and Hindu prayer flags. The front porch was deep and well-covered with a roof that had woven bamboo screens hanging from it. Despite the lightly falling snow—it was too warm for the snow to stick—a huge, furry mutt, maybe part Bernese Mountain Dog, part bear, looked plenty warm on his overstuffed plaid dog bed by the front door. He lifted his nose and sniffed at Jane's boots. She had to agree, flowered rain boots weren't quite the thing.

Gemma rang the bell. She greeted the girl who answered the door with a big hug and kiss and handed her a bottle of something in a paper sack. Jane knew that Christians liked their beer and wine in Portland, but the idea of a drinking kind of party made her stomach tighten. She'd never been to one before. If she didn't drink, would everyone think she was a snob? If she did, would she make an idiot of herself, get horribly sick, and disappoint God? She gritted her teeth. Maybe there wasn't actual drinking inside. Just a nice wine bottle as a hostess gift?

Gemma gave Jane a little push into the house. Everyone seemed to have a glass of wine or a bottle of something in their hands. It was definitely a drinking kind of party, and, as she looked around the room, she found that she didn't know anyone at all.

Jane wandered over to the snack table and piled a plate with stuffed mushrooms, crackers topped with pimento cheese, and some kind of dinner roll thing stuffed with something that smelled good. She grabbed a bottle of water from the cooler on the floor and slunk back to a wall to eat and be miserable.

Gemma bounced from group to group. She hugged a redhead with dark brown lipstick and then held her at arm's length, complimenting her dress. She introduced herself to a tall man with grey hair and black glasses, handsome, if you were into older men. Then she wandered into another room without a backwards glance at Jane.

Jane heard Gemma explode into laughter from the other room, even though the general buzz of conversation was pretty loud. She crunched a cracker and considered the scene. She'd bet that somewhere in the crowd, someone had a bad secret. As a potential future missionary, it was good to be able to determine which person in a group had a need that Christ could meet. As a detective in training, the ability to tell who was hiding something was invaluable.

She stopped.

Isaac wasn't anywhere in the room. She didn't need to lean against the wall justifying her two passions to him.

She took a deep breath and stepped into the kitchen to see what else was happening at the random party Gemma had found out about through Twitter.

For the millionth time since Christmas day, a tall man with short brown hair made her catch her breath.

She slowly exhaled. Someday she'd stop thinking she saw him in every crowd.

Then he laughed.

Jane stepped back through the door.

What was Isaac doing here?

Before she could decide to run outside and catch a bus home, the hostess weaved her way through the kitchen. "Everyone gather, gather around! It's time for traditional solstice games!"

Jane followed the hostess out and hoped Isaac wouldn't notice her.

Most of the guests gathered in the front room. The hostess grinned, her cherry-red lips a bright spot in a room that had grown oppressive to Jane. "This is my traditional English winter solstice after-party! We're going to play a couple of traditional games, then have crackers, and maybe, if everyone is good, Father Christmas will come!" She giggled, just a little. She was tipsy, but not totally wasted. "First game: sardines. Does everyone know how to play?"

Laughter spilled across the crowd. The grey-haired man Gemma had introduced herself to groaned. The girl next to Jane, also wearing rain boots, snickered.

"This is a big house. I'm going to turn out all the lights. You all stay here, with your eyes closed. Count to thirty while I hide. You all have to find me. When you find me, though, you have to hide with me! Got it? Last person to hide with us loses."

Jane tried to stare at her hostess's cherry-red lips, but it was impossible because Isaac Daniels was standing right behind her, to the left, staring at her with his big hazel eyes. And he looked sad.

Then the lights went out.

All of them.

The room was crowded and dark. It smelled like cinnamon candles, Christmas trees, vanilla incense, and Jake.

"Hang in there, kiddo. You can make it through this." Jake's voice was a whisper in her ear.

She reached behind her and found his hand.

He gripped it. "I don't know who invited him, but don't go thinking it's fate just because you are both here." His words were quiet, and he was very close.

She nodded, and felt his lips moving against her ear. "I invited Gemma. I'm sorry. I knew if I did, she'd bring you. But I wouldn't have done it if I had known that weird Daniels kid would be here."

Jake led her by the hand into the kitchen. It was also completely dark.

"I need to go home," Jane whispered. The house was buzzing with whispers and quiet laughter, but overall, the spirit of the game was in full effect and the creaking floorboards were louder now than the voices.

"Don't go home." Jake stroked the back of her hand with his thumb. "Please?"

Jane closed her eyes. She couldn't see his face and didn't want her eyes to adjust to the dark so she could. She wanted him to keep holding her hand, and keep treating her like she mattered.

She wanted him to kiss her.

She wanted him to wrap his arms around her, pull her close, and kiss her so that if Isaac wandered into the room, she wouldn't even notice.

Jake dropped her hand. "I can take you home, if you want." His voice was flat.

"No…don't."

He stepped forward, his face close to hers again, his cheek brushing hers. "That's my girl."

If she turned her head just a fraction, she would kiss him.

And Gemma's heart would break.

Jane kept perfectly still.

"Do you want to go find our hostess, or sit in the living room like civilized Americans drinking Dr. Pepper and talking about work?"

Jane felt like her spine was frozen. She couldn't turn her head, not even if she wanted to. "I haven't played sardines since junior high youth group."

"Then let's go find Heather." Jake grabbed her hand again and led her around the kitchen.

He twined his fingers through hers. A jolt of electricity sped from her fingertips through her whole body. The room was unbearably warm, but she couldn't let go…or she wouldn't be able to follow him around in the dark.

"I went to Michelle Smith's old school," Jane whispered. She didn't want Jake to be her rebound boyfriend. He was too good of a friend for that. She had to talk about the case before her panic made her ruin a good thing.

"What did you learn?"

"There's at least one family there that might want to see harm come to her."

"Really?" Jake stopped.

Jane kept going and bumped into him.

He put his arm around her waist and led her to a far corner. He kept his voice low and his mouth near her ear, but not quite so intimately close as before. "What's the motive?"

She took one step too many and bumped him with her knees. "They lost a lawsuit for back tuition and fees. The court ordered they pay up. Including legal fees, they owe her one hundred thousand."

Jake let out a low whistle. He tightened his grip on her waist. "Well done."

"I also learned that the security guard on duty that night is now on administrative leave, and that the room is monitored, so whatever he did…for example, if he left his post…has been recorded."

"Interesting. Does he have any ties to the victim?"

"Nothing I've found yet. I'm still waiting to hear back from his girlfriend. She works security there too." Talking about the case in whispers didn't help calm her down. Every word he whispered felt like code, and every word she said felt like a promise.

"Have you worked out her connection to the protesters yet?" Jake couldn't get any closer. She could feel the bristles of his unshaved face on her cheek.

"Not yet. I need to get ahold of the reporter too. Remember her? She and a cameraman were everywhere that night. They must have seen something. Maybe even recorded it."

"I've got that contact. Let me get in touch with her."

Jane's heart flipped. He could know the kind-of-famous, and very pretty, news reporter. Why not? It didn't matter to her.

"You're going to crack this open, Jane." He pulled her around so they were face-to-face.

Her heart beat so hard she knew he could hear it. His nose bumped hers.

"Jane…" He leaned forward, just enough to bridge the hairsbreadth distance between his lips and hers, but she turned her head.

He leaned his forehead on hers. "You hardly knew him. You hadn't seen him in six months." He wrapped his other arm around her. Both arms embracing her, hiding her away. "He never called while he was in Costa Rica. Then, just a month after that, he moved to Montreal." His whisper was soft, inviting.

"But…" She didn't have an answer.

"It's not a rebound if it's real love."

She rested her forehead on his shoulder.

He ran his fingers through her hair.

"Are you the sardine?" The whisperer had a deep voice and stuffed-up nose.

A girl giggled. "Did we find Heather in the breakfast nook?"

Several people pushed into the corner, pressing Jane into Jake. He tightened his arm around her. "See?" He tilted her face up with his thumb. “We’re predestined to do this.” He laughed, a deep, throaty chuckle, and kissed her, full on the lips, with people pressed around them in the dark.

She melted, from the top of her head to her toes. She thought she would slip through his arms into a puddle on the floor.

The light turned on.

Someone laughed.

Jane’s eyes flew open.

Jake stopped kissing her, but didn’t let go.

“Sorry! I just wanted to get the paper towels!” A red-faced woman with a Christmas light necklace that actually lit up laughed nervously. “Those rugs in there are antique.” She grabbed for a roll of paper towels on the counter.

The man who had been jostling Jane with his elbows grabbed Jake by the shoulders and shoved him across the room. “Get your hands off of her!” It was Isaac. He pushed Jake again, this time into the kitchen table.

Jake pulled himself up and sat on the table, a silly grin plastered on his face. “Hold your horses, cowboy.”

“What do you think you’re doing?” Isaac pushed him with his fingertips. Jake wobbled, but kept his seat.

“Kissing Jane. Did you not see?”

Isaac reeled back and swung. His fist cracked against Jake’s nose with a burst of blood.

"Isaac!" Jane screamed. She grabbed his arm and pulled him back.

"You were going to marry me, Jane. You were still going to marry me." He brushed his eyes with the back of his hand. "We had one dumb fight. That was all. It was going to be all right." Isaac wavered. He looked at his bloody fist and then at Jane.

"Have you been drinking?" Jane stepped back.

Two women pressed wet towels to Jake's face.

"Isaac, have you been drinking?" She grabbed his arms in clenched fingers and stared at him.

"Maybe. Why wouldn't I be? This Christmas is a nightmare." He wrenched his arms out of her hands.

"Go home, Isaac. Walk it off." She stared at him. His face was burning red, and droplets of blood from breaking Jake's nose were splattered across his white shirt.

"You still love me." He used his teacher voice. Like it was an assignment.

"I don't even know you." She swallowed. Nausea overwhelmed her.

Isaac's face softened, and one tear escaped.

Her head spun. Isaac was broken. Completely brokenhearted. She touched his sleeve.

"I still love you." Isaac's voice was different now. Not fighting. Not demanding. Just sad.

"You don't know me."

"Can someone drive Jake to the hospital?" an older female voice asked.

Jane looked over Isaac's shoulder.

Jake was staring at her, one eyebrow raised, half a smile on his face, a wet towel slowly turning pink pressed to his nose.

"I'll dribe byself." Jake hopped off the table.

"Don't." Jane reached for Jake, but he just smiled and ambled out of the kitchen. "Is he okay to drive?" Jane looked around the room, trying to catch someone's eye.

The girl nearest her shrugged. "Sure."

"He seems fine. They'll stitch him up." The older woman, not that old really, but with a tired, gravelly voice, waved her glass at Jane and then left the kitchen as well.

Jane spun around ready to yell at Isaac, but he had managed to slip out.

Instead, she found Gemma. Crying.

"I'm so sorry." Jane stepped forward, her hand out to comfort her in some way.

Gemma scrunched her face up. "Whatever." She pushed her way through the rest of the guests and left.

Jane stared around the room. A few girls snuck a look at her, then looked away, but mostly people were more interested in their own thing than in her. She slumped against the wall.

It would stink to walk all the way home in her rain boots.

CHAPTER 13

THE SNOW FELL IN SOFT, DUST-LIKE FLAKES that shone white under the streetlights. It was a dry, cold snow, but the ground was wet from recent rain and the flakes melted on contact. Jane watched them from her seat under the bus shelter. She had walked as far as the bus shelter in her rain boots when she decided that the hot, stinky bus was better than the cold, dark night.

"Why Jake Crawford?" Isaac took a seat next to Jane on the bench.

"Been walking around in the dark?" Jane tapped her toes in rapid staccato.

"Yes." Isaac ran his hands through his hair. "But I wasn't drinking. I was just really mad. I don't like that I got so mad, but…"

She knocked his knee with her fist. "You were pretty mad."

"You were kissing Jake."

"Yeah."

"Again." Isaac stared into the street as he spoke.

"Yeah."

"Has it always been Jake?"

Jane shook her head. "No." She paused. "I don't know. He's a good friend. You were a long-distance boyfriend. Long distance is hard."

"Yeah."

She reached for his hand. "I can't marry you, because you don't want to be married to me. You want to be married to a girl who seems like me but has a different personality."

"I don't see it like that."

"I know." Jane tipped her head back so it rested against the plastic wall of the bus shelter.

"It's only ten. Want to go get something to eat?"

"No. I want to go home and make Gemma feel better."

"Jane…I don't want to give up."

"We can't make this work. You're too…" She chewed on her cheek. What was he? She was tempted to say too perfect, but she really meant he thought he was too perfect.

"What?"

"You're too not right for me. I have a dream, and a plan, and a hope, and your dream doesn't have room for any of those. I can't give up all of that for something I don't want."

Isaac stood up. "The bus is coming."

Jane saw it down the road, just a couple of blocks away. "I'm sorry about not answering your calls."

"Doesn't matter."

"It was rude."

The bus pulled up.

"I'm going..." Jane pointed at the bus.

"Yeah." Isaac narrowed his eyes, but looked away.

"Montreal..." The bus door folded open. "Just...enjoy it. It's your dream." She climbed into the bus. From her seat, she watched him as the bus pulled away.

He walked slowly, eyes to the ground.

At the apartment, Gemma paced the living room. Her hands were clasped behind her back, and her eyes were red and swollen. "You know how I feel about him, and you didn't even want to give me a chance."

"You invited Isaac to the party, didn't you?"

"You're an idiot for leaving him. He's nice, handsome, has a good job. What are you thinking?"

Jane pressed her lips together. "He is nice, and handsome, and has a good job, but so are hundreds of other men in the world I'm not going to marry."

"You shouldn't ruin your friendship with Jake this way." Gemma paused in front of the window and crossed her arms. Her brows were pulled down over her eyes.

"I agree."

"So what are you going to do about it?" Gemma's whole body quivered.

"I don't know." The apartment seemed small with Gemma so angry. Jane grabbed her purse and went back out. She drove past her aunt's house, but it was pretty late, and Jane was fairly sure Aunt May would take her daughter's side. She drove past the library and really wished it was open twenty-four hours. She drove past the Miramontes, a small, fancy hotel not far from her apartment, but even if she did have an expense fund from Jake burning a hole in her pocket, she didn't think it would be a wise use of money.

She drove to the big Crawford house and stared at the dark windows.

The front porch light flicked on.

Jane whapped her head against the steering wheel. Why did he have to be home already?

Phoebe Crawford, Jake's sister, came running down the steps, wrapped only in a silky robe. She knocked on the window of Jane's car. "Are you coming in or not?" she asked. "It's cold out here."

Jane followed Phoebe into the house.

They stopped in the front living room, which was almost exactly the same as it had been when Jane was cleaning it. A little messier, but mostly the same.

Jane slumped onto the loveseat.

Phoebe lounged in a wingback chair. "The important question now is: what are you going to do about it?"

"You heard?"

"Uh, yes. Jake's not going to let a war wound go uncommented on, is he?"

Jane checked her watch. "But he'd hardly be out of the emergency room yet. It's only been an hour and a half."

"He called." Phoebe shrugged. "He took a hit for you. How will you repay him?"

Jane stared at the ceiling. "Is it wrong to say that I don't know?"

Phoebe slid onto the couch and crossed her long legs. "You don't have a lot of experience with this, do you?"

"Nope."

"Was Isaac your first boyfriend?'

Jane smiled, embarrassed. "There was another guy, back in high school, but…"

"Isaac was your first. And you just dumped him, and you feel like it's breaking some kind of important code to immediately replace him with someone you like better."

Jane took a deep breath. "Yes."

"And you feel guilty for liking Jake better because if Isaac had lived here, you probably would have liked *him* better."

Jane lifted her eyebrows.

"Years and years of therapy, Jane. I may only be twenty, but I've got more meds on my chart and more therapy under my belt than the Real Housewives of New York."

Jane looked away.

"It's okay, really. It's a good thing. You wouldn't rather my bipolar disorder go untreated for all these years, would you?" She laughed.

Jane smiled. "I'm sorry. I'm confused. I don't know where to start."

"Start like this: how hot is Liam Hemsworth on a scale of one to one hundred?"

"Uhh..." Jane scrunched her face.

"Okay then, Joseph Gordon-Levitt?"

Jane grinned. "Ninety-nine point five?"

"Exactly. Cute, charming, talented. But you don't know him, do you?"

"Nope."

"Because he doesn't live here. He's an actor, not whatever it is you are. And your paths won't cross—ever. You might like him way more than Isaac if you ever met him, but will you? Nope. Would you move to LA so you could meet him and make him love you?"

"No." Jane saw where this was going, but it wasn't the same. She had met Isaac, and she...

"Earth to Jane. Don't abandon the conversation. It's important. Maybe you would like Isaac or Joseph Gordon-Levitt more than Jake, but what good does that do? They aren't a part of your life. Not a real part."

"I get it, but it's a stretch."

"Okay then, back to good old Joseph G-L. How hot do you think he is?"

Jane laughed. "He's my type."

"Exactly. He was the actor who looked and acted the most like Jake that I could think of." Phoebe stood up. "I'm going to bed. I'm glad we got this sorted."

Taking love advice from Jake's surprisingly insightful sister…another new experience to chalk up for the year. She curled up and closed her eyes. Apparently Phoebe was okay with her spending the night.

"Psst, Jane."

Jane pressed her face into the pillow. It couldn't be morning yet. She turned and peeled one eye open. It was still dark.

"Wake up, just a little." Jake pushed her shoulder.

Jane rolled onto her side and hugged the throw pillow to her chest. Jake had a bandage across his nose and bruises under his eyes. She reached out and touched his bandage, just barely. "Did Isaac break you?"

"Only fair. You broke him, after all."

She stroked Jake's hair. "Poor Isaac."

Jake leaned back against the couch.

"I thought you didn't live here anymore."

"I don't, but it was closer than home, and, to be honest, this kind of hurts."

Jane kissed his cheek. "It looks like it does."

Jake wrapped her hand in both of his. "I don't ever want you to leave that couch. But I also don't want to rush you—which is a lie. I do want to rush you. But I won't."

Jane sniffled. She didn't know exactly what she was sniffling about, but the tears were coming anyway. Good girls didn't jump from man to man like this.

"You're really close to my ear right now, and that snot-slurping thing you just did was disgusting, but I still want to kiss you. That's how I know it is love."

Jane laughed. "I keep running to you when things are hard. Or when they are good."

"And that's how *you* know it is love."

Jane didn't respond, but he was right.

"We're family, Jane. Not kissing cousins or anything weird like that. Just family. It's meant to be."

"Maybe so."

"I'd better not tempt fate." Jake kissed the back of her hand, and left.

CHAPTER 14

ROSE OF SHARON FINALLY RESPONDED to Jane's earlier Facebook message to get together at Sprouted Quinoa. She had also friended Jane on Facebook. They were to meet for breakfast at nine, which gave Jane plenty of time to read everything Rose of Sharon had posted. There were a dozen posts about the Fro-Yo Murder, and how a good woman had given her life for the cause.

Would Rose of Sharon murder to create a martyr?

Jane went to the little vegan restaurant with all senses on alert.

Rose of Sharon was smaller up close than Jane had expected. She was no taller than Jane, in fact. Five three and a half at the most.

Rose of Sharon took Jane's hand in hers and held it for a moment. Her skin was papery like an older woman's, but warm. "Thank you so much for coming here to meet me."

They sat in a small booth at the back of the restaurant. "How are you holding up?" Jane's heart twinged with sympathy. Rose of Sharon's eyes were red and her signature curly hair was pulled back into a bun.

"Michelle was a good woman. Stabbing is a painful way to die."

"I can't think of worse." Jane sipped her kefir. "How long was Michelle a Helper?"

Rose of Sharon wiped her eyes with an unbleached cotton napkin. "She wasn't. We were just friends."

"I had heard…"

"I know. That's a problem I have. My girls went to Trillium. I have a deep respect for Michelle, and we were friends. But she wasn't a protester."

"When were your kids at Trillium?" Jane was writing as she spoke, but Rose of Sharon didn't seem put off by it.

"Clover was there ten years ago, and Isis was there about fifteen."

"Michelle supported the work of HLP though, didn't she?"

"She was a kindred spirit, for sure, but she was never involved in any protest."

"Could any of the protesters have had a problem with her? Maybe they thought she was benefitting from the work and from her friendship without giving back in return."

Rose of Sharon picked up a wafer that Jane didn't recognize and nibbled it. "Maybe." She put her food down. "The Human Liberation Party is not as organized as people on the outside think. We meet like flash mobs do, and always have. We don't have an official roster or membership list. I can't vouch for everyone who calls themselves a Helper."

"Do you wish it was different?"

Rose of Sharon nodded.

"Really?" Jane raised an eyebrow.

Rose of Sharon smiled and rolled her eyes. "I know it doesn't seem like it from the news, but I do like a bit of organization in my work. You might have noticed that when I rally, it is an organized event. We meet at a specific time and place. We have a specific mission, a goal to meet before we disband. You can change the world a lot faster with a plan."

"I admit, that does surprise me."

"Listen, I have a master's degree in community organization and a doctorate in human development. I wrote the seminal thesis on whole foods, the developing world, and American obesity. My thesis is taught to university students around the world."

An idea was growing in Jane's mind, but she wasn't sure if it was a good one. "How did Michelle feed the kids at the preschool?"

Rose of Sharon frowned. "I sent food with my kids."

"But how did she feed everyone else?"

"I couldn't say, really. I think it was good, though." Rose of Sharon looked over Jane's shoulder.

She was lying.

Jane moved on. "How well do you know a Helper called Valeria?"

"Valeria Bean? She's the daughter of an old friend."

"How is she holding up? She seemed really upset at the event."

"Oh…" Rose of Sharon exhaled slowly. "She's not doing well at all. I don't know why. I guess she's just very tenderhearted."

"There was another Helper sitting with her. He seemed very protective. Young guy, dark hair. Would you know who that was?"

"Probably her husband, Yuri."

"It was really good she had him there, I think." Jane sipped her kefir again.

"Jane…can I call you Jane? I wish you wouldn't do that in front of me."

"Excuse me?"

"The kefir. I just think it's really insensitive of you to drink that after all that we've gone through."

"Because it's dairy? But it's been fermented." Jane held the drink at arm's length. It was truly repulsive, but it had sounded healthy, so she ordered.

"Please. That's just an excuse to feed a dairy addiction."

Jane took another drink. She gagged a little. "It's really gross."

Rose of Sharon laughed. "God made food to give us pleasure. Not to gross us out." She nibbled the grey-green wafer. "This one is gross too."

"Rose of Sharon…I'm confused."

"Good. If you're confused, you're thinking. Don't put me in a box because I won't eat hamburgers. I want to honor my body. It's a temple of God. I want you to do the same thing." She stood up. "I need to get to work, but if I can help you in any way, I will. I cared about Michelle, and am devastated that she died the way she did."

Rose of Sharon left Jane sitting with the kefir, the tray of raw-food spreads and wafers, and a bowl of fruit. But she didn't leave Jane with the bill.

Valeria and Yuri had acted suspicious after the murder. Perhaps Valeria had been sensitive, or maybe she had seen her husband cozy up to Michelle at the wrong time.

Before Jane left, she spent some time on her phone, exploring Rose of Sharon's Facebook friends. She found Valeria Bean, and learned that she worked at a local pet store. Companions was across town, but Jane went straight there.

She recognized the nervous, skinny woman with the dishwater curls behind the counter right away. Before she spoke with her, she toured the stop. Mostly natural and niche pet supplies, but there was also a beautiful selection of birds and fish. One tank had about a dozen clown fish in it.

After her brief tour, Jane joined Valeria at the cash register. "Hey there." She decided to give Valeria a chance to recognize her from the event, but it didn't seem to work.

"Good morning." Valeria smiled, but not with her eyes. She seemed distracted.

"Valeria…my name is Jane. I met you at the fundraiser you were protesting the day after Christmas."

"Okay." Valeria's face blanched.

"Right now I'm working as a private detective to help solve the murder of Michelle Smith. I remember that you were pretty shaken up that night. Did you see something while you were there?"

Valeria chewed her lip. Her cheeks slowly turned red. "No."

"Please, Valeria. Did you see anything at all? A really nice person died that night."

"I don't know what I saw. It was such a crowded room."

"Did you see someone get really angry? One of the guests, maybe?"

Valeria leaned forward. "I didn't see anything." Her voice was a hoarse whisper, and she emphasized the word "see."

Jane lowered her voice as well. "But you heard something?"

Valeria nodded.

"Anything you saw or heard, anything could help."

Valeria looked around. Her coworker was helping another customer at the clown fish tank. “I heard the TV news reporter say something scary. It really scared me, but I can’t remember exactly what it was now. Do you know what I mean?”

Jane’s heart sank. She had had those times, when she couldn’t trust her own memory. “What do you think you heard?”

“The reporter was talking to a man in a black sweater. He looked mean, narrow eyed. She was quiet, but she was standing close to me.”

“What did she say?”

Valeria took a deep breath. “Remember, I don’t know if this was really it or not. She said, ‘Do it now while the cameraman is in the bathroom.’”

Jane wrote it down. “Do what? Did you watch the man in the sweater to see what he would do?”

Valeria nodded. “I did, but he just meandered his way through the crowd. I lost sight of him pretty quickly.”

“Valeria…” Jane kept her voice very low. “How long after this did the woman scream?”

A tear rolled down Valeria’s cheek. “About five minutes.”

Jane exhaled a breath she had been holding. “You knew the man in the black sweater, didn’t you?”

Valeria shook her head. “No, I didn’t, I swear I didn’t know him.”

Jane drummed her fingers on the counter. "Are you absolutely sure?"

"I didn't know him…" Valeria exhaled slowly. "But Rose of Sharon did. Way earlier, when we were still outside, she saw him. They hugged."

"Did she say his name?"

Valeria shook her head. "She called him 'buddy.' I wish she had said his name."

"Do me a favor, please, Valeria. Please, tell the police what you heard. I know it's not much, and you might be scared, but they need to know everything."

Valeria nodded. "I need to?"

"Please, please do."

Jane left with a stone in her heart. She was getting closer to the killer now, but it wasn't pretty.

Jane had to clean two houses before she could get back to detecting. But as soon as she was done, she drove by Ben's house. He had finally responded to her text with a halfhearted comment about how he would try and see if he could help.

Ben let her in. He was dressed in sweats and a T-shirt. The house looked like a girl had exploded in it, which kind of shocked Jane until she remembered that Ben had gotten married a couple of years ago. He cut straight to the chase.

"'Bang-Bang Bambi's dead' is a name this user created just for this thread. The poster also uses 'HuntingisZombieTargetPractice' and just plain 'Shoot.'"

"But what's his real name?"

Ben smiled. "How much is it worth to you?"

Jane sighed.

"I'm kidding. His real name is Ethan Franklin-Miter."

Miter? That couldn't be a coincidence.

"What else did you learn about Ethan? Age? Location? School? Work?"

"He doesn't have a LinkedIn, a Facebook, or a Twitter, none of that."

"So he's not a professional, and he is younger than…twenty-five?"

"He doesn't play on Ask.com and he doesn't have a Tumblr."

"Older than thirteen but younger than eighteen?"

"That'd be my guess. So take whatever he says with a grain of salt."

"I've already confirmed his claim. Actually, he was wrong, but it was the kind of mistake a kid would make, I think."

"So you can leave the kid alone now? It felt really wrong cyber stalking a kid."

Jane scratched her ear. "Yeah, I can leave Ethan alone. But…"

"I don't care what you do with his parents. Just leave the kid alone."

"Of course, of course. Thanks for your help, Ben."

"No problem. Just remember me when you want a hot new private detective website, okay?"

"Absolutely."

Jane drove straight to Jake's office. He had his own work to do, of course, but he might be able to help her put her new pieces together.

He was with someone in the office. Jane decided not to interrupt this time. She went back downstairs to the restaurant and had a late lunch while she went over her notes.

The list of what she needed to learn was still a longer list than what she already knew. To start with: Who was the man in the black sweater? How did the reporter know him? Why would the reporter want Michelle Smith dead? Then there was the weirder issue of Del the security guy. Why had he been put on admin leave?

Jane pulled up YouTube on her phone while she waited for Jake. She scrolled through the local news until she found the reporter from that night. Her name was Myra Richardson. Or at least, that was her television name. Jane wondered if perhaps, her real name was Myra Miter…

Jane poked at her chicken salad. She needed an in with the television station so she could talk to Myra—and about Myra.

She thought Jake had mentioned her being his contact, but he didn't seem to have connected with her yet.

She considered the connections she had made with her housecleaning business, but she couldn't think of anyone who had ties to television.

From the corner of her eye, Jane spotted Jake. He stood in the doorway, the pale winter sun shining on him. Sandy hair. Red plaid scarf. Wooly businessman winter coat. He didn't really look like Joseph Gordon-Levitt, except when he smiled.

He was smiling.

The good news was that they had a case to solve while they figured out if they were a thing or not.

The bad news was Gemma.

She wished she hadn't tried to set them up.

Jake joined her at the table. He slung his coat across the back of his chair to reveal a retro raglan-sleeved Roly Burger company shirt. "This thing with the mayor is going to send me to an early grave." He ran his fingers through his short hair. "Between blue laws and fro-yo murders, I don't know what I'm going to do."

Jane set her phone down. "Tell me what's going on."

"Frozen yogurt is a weak commodity in the winter anyway, but we're also new to town, not as much fun as the fro-yo with the candy toppings bar, and now with the 'Fro-Yo Murder' label." Jake shuddered. "Have you heard the new one? 'Local

Frozen Yogurt Fundraiser Sends Children's Advocate to Yo-*Heaven*.'"

"That's atrocious." Jane pushed her salad away. "No one really said that."

Jake picked up Jane's phone and pulled up the local news.

Jane read the headline. "That's, that's…"

"Exactly. There are no words." Jake swallowed, his Adam's apple moving up and down. "I don't know that I can keep the business alive."

"Don't say that." Jane rested her hand on Jake's elbow.

"This Roly Burger—the second-to-last Roly Burger, since I converted my Portland location to a Yo-Heaven over the summer—does great business on the weekends. If the blue laws take effect…" He shook his head.

"It can't take effect before Christmas, anyway."

Jake shrugged.

"So let's get a Christmas tree in here. We'll do events every weekend. Coloring contests, gifts. Freebies. Charity giveaways."

Jake took a deep breath. "That's a lot of work."

"And let's get the murder solved. Get the 'Fro-Yo Murder' out of the headlines and business will perk back up."

Jake's face was stony. "I don't want to see my managers have to make layoffs."

"Then tell them not to."

"I will, for now. We can float everyone for a little while." Jake leaned forward and lowered his voice. "I don't think I'm doing a very good job as president of the Crawford family restaurant outfit."

Jane chewed on her lip. Running her little housecleaning business was not the same as running the restaurant empire. "Do you have a good mentor?"

"I've got Aunt Marge and Jeff."

"Who's Jeff?"

"He's my cousin. And the man that should be running the business. He's like forty and worked for my dad forever."

Jane squeezed his arm. Young heir. Experienced cousin. Cousin who would have been the heir if only Jake's uncle had been the oldest Crawford son. "Just keep begging him for help. He doesn't want to see you fail."

"Good old Jane." Jake picked her hand up and kissed it. "Until I can bend Jeff's ear again, I need to be proactive. So let's solve the murder."

Jane laid out everything she had learned from both Rose of Sharon and Valeria.

"So who was the man in the black sweater?" Jake asked.

"It may have been Del, the security guy. Except Valeria saw him arrive, so it must have been the Miter guy who owed Michelle so much money."

"Why would Myra Richardson of KMLC want to help someone kill a perfectly innocent preschool teacher?" Jake stole a piece of crispy chicken from Jane's salad and munched it.

"Maybe her maiden name is Miter." Jane lifted an eyebrow. This one theory seemed to tie everything else together.

"Nope. I used to date her kid sister Josie. They're the Kerseys from Government Camp."

"So no relation to the Miters at all?" Jane's heart sunk. She wasn't sure which was worse: that Jake had dated the younger sister of the beautiful reporter, or that the reporter wasn't really Myra Miter.

"I can't be sure that there's no relation, but there's definitely no close relation. She's not the sister of or daughter of."

"But…" Jane felt the first real glimpse of hope shining through the disappointment. Jake had dated Myra's sister Josie. He knew Myra personally. "You've got an in with Myra. You could call her and find out who the man in the black sweater was!"

"Uh…" Jake pulled up a new video on Jane's phone. It was a news clip from the night in question. Myra was talking.

"Notorious playboy Jake Crawford is trying to rehabilitate the increasingly shaky reputation of his family restaurant business by holding a fundraiser for a start-up nonprofit."

Jane rolled her eyes. “So much for impartial reporting. What did you do to her?”

“I dumped her sister.” Jake gave an apologetic half-smile.

“For who, her bestie?”

“For you.”

“Ahh, jeeze. So neither of us can use your connection then.”

“Nope.”

“Wait. You had already dumped her by the night of the fundraiser? I only broke it off with Isaac the night before.”

“I dumped her last year, when you moved in with me.” He winked.

Jane laughed. “You have got to stop saying that or everyone will get the wrong idea.” She had known he was interested back then, but…she hadn’t known he meant it. She felt heat rising to her cheeks.

“I’ll call her anyway.” Jake resumed his serious expression. “If I suggest what we found out looks bad, and she remembers all the nasty things she said about me on TV, I might be able to get something good out of her.”

“It’s worth a shot, anyway.”

Jake tapped the screen of his phone. He grinned. “Jake Crawford, notorious playboy, how can I help you?”

Jane lowered her eyes and hid her laugh behind her hand. But she listened in to his side of the call.

"Oh, no hard feelings, of course. It's only had forty-two thousand hits on YouTube. That's not at all grounds for a defamation case." Jake laughed. "No, no. I think we can work something out." There was a long pause. Jake rolled his eyes. "Off the record? What's that even mean? I wouldn't be calling if I didn't need to know something." Another pause. This time Jake ate more of Jane's lunch. "I see. Well, I could do that. But I would feel more inclined if you helped me out, on the record." His eyes lit up. "You always were a good girl. So, here's the thing. One of the protesters heard you chatting with someone that we need to meet. We just don't know his name." Jake inhaled sharply. "Nothing like that. I think you said, 'The cameraman is in the bathroom, go do it now.' Or something similar. You were talking to a man in a black sweater." Jake narrowed his eyes. "Well…I guess that would be easy enough to check. Are you sure though? We don't want a guess here. We want his real name." Jake frowned and rolled his eyes in exasperation. "Okay. Yeah. I'll look into it and see if he was telling the truth." Jake made a face like something stunk. "Call my assistant and she'll see if she can fit you in." He ended the call.

Jane sat on the edge of her chair. Her heart was racing. "Well?"

"She said she met him that night. He asked for a moment of her time when he noticed the camera was gone. She said he wanted to make a big donation, but wanted to do it anonymously. He wanted to be absolutely certain that he wasn't on camera."

Jane slumped back in her chair. "And she didn't get his name?"

"No, she did. His name was Jason Miter."

CHAPTER 15

JANE AND JAKE WENT STRAIGHT BACK UPSTAIRS to go over the donation receipts. If Miter had wanted to be completely anonymous, they might be in trouble, but if he had written a check, they could prove he had been telling the truth. If there wasn't a check, then they had to consider any particularly large cash donation as potential evidence.

Jane's Aunt May had been manning the donations for the night and kept meticulous notes of everything that came to her. Jane thanked God they hadn't just let Gemma handle that. If there weren't any particularly large cash donations, or checks from the Miter family, then there was a chance he had been lying and wanted to know he could sidle up to Michelle Smith without being seen. Jane shuddered. It was a particularly repulsive killer who could viciously murder someone in a crowded room.

Of course, she had to admit that he might have left a big donation and still have killed Michelle Smith.

The list of donations was in a small, hardbound accounts book. Jane leaned over Jake's shoulder to read it with him.

He spun in his desk chair and pulled Jane to his lap. He wrapped his arms around her waist and nibbled her neck.

"This isn't helping." Her heart thumped, and she was suddenly too hot in her sweater.

"Yes, it is."

His lips on her neck were like nothing else. Like chocolate, and coffee, and everything. She took a deep breath. "No, really. It's not helping." She stood up.

Jake grinned. "You. That's all. Just, you." He took a deep breath. "What were we doing?"

"You…receipts. Me…sitting far, far away from you." She took a chair across the room, but couldn't take her eyes off of him.

His lips were curled in the smallest hint of a smile, just enough to make a dimple in his cheek. He caught her eye and winked. She wanted to concentrate on important things. Whatever those were.

She pulled up Beth from security's phone number and called.

"Beth! Hey, this is Jane, the detective."

Jake winked at her.

"I was just wondering if you had any news on Del."

"Oh, I do! I can't tell you how relieved I am." Beth's voice sounded relaxed and happy. Jane was thrilled for her, but wanted her to get to the point.

"Good news then?"

"Great news. He didn't have a girl in the room at all."

"That is good." Jane tapped her heel. "What was the problem?"

Beth dropped her voice. "He's pretty sure he disposed of the murder weapon."

Jane almost dropped her phone. "What?"

"He slipped out to use the bathroom, which is totally against the rules if you are in the box alone. Some guy saw him come out of the security room and followed him into the bathroom. He kind of, like, threatened him, you know? Like, said he'd tell the boss and get Del fired if he didn't take this huge Hefty bag of garbage and put it on the curb at his house."

Red flags flew up all over the story. Jane grabbed a pencil and started writing. "How did the man know Del wasn't supposed to go to the bathroom?"

"He asked a bunch of questions first. Del wasn't supposed to be alone, but there was, like, an hour or something when he was. It happens sometimes. The guy kind of chatted him up, discovered what he needed to know, and then made him take the bag."

"Did Del do it?"

"Sort of. He stuck it in a bathroom stall and was going to take it home. He thought it must have had some kind of drugs stuff in it, like used needles or something. But when he got back from the bathroom, obviously there was chaos at the party and he was pretty sure he knew what had happened. He got Lafayette on the walkie and confessed all, but when they went to the bathroom, the bag was gone. She had to put him on admin leave."

Jane scratched her head and frowned. "He gave the description of the guy to the cops, right?"

"Of course."

"But why did he show up to work again and lie to you about the admin leave?"

Beth laughed softly. "He was really embarrassed. I shouldn't say anything, but he has a juvie record that I didn't know about until now. This just hit too close to home, and he panicked."

"I see." Juvenile criminal record, eh? Maybe the man with the bag was a lie to cover the murder?

"My bus just got here. I've got to go. I hope that helped."

"Wait—do you think I can talk to Del? I'd love to hear his description of the guy who gave him the bag."

"That's not a good idea. He really doesn't want to talk about it. Have a great day, okay?" Beth hung up.

Through the whole conversation, Beth had been fairly relaxed. She had a twinge of emotion when she mentioned Del's record, but overall, she had come across as entirely honest. So at the very least she was reporting exactly what Del had said. Unfortunately, Jane had failed, yet again, to get Del's last name.

"I found the donation." Jake sounded disappointed. "Twenty thousand dollars from Miter Farms to Helping Hands E. C."

"Who invited Jason Miter to the fundraiser?" Jane sat on the edge of Jake's desk, across from him.

"That's anyone's guess. He's not on my list or Gemma's. Until now, I'd never heard of him."

"Do you think Sasha might have invited him to force him to interact with Michelle?"

"Maybe. Why don't you call her and ask?"

Jane had Sasha's number up on her phone almost immediately, but she had to leave a message. She filled in the gaps of her conversation with Beth. "What do you think, Jake? Do we trust Del's account?"

"I think we need to confirm it with the security boss."

"Did you see anyone taking trash out in the middle of our party?"

"No, remember, almost as soon as Michelle was stabbed, we had the room organized and ready for the cops. Nobody came or went. I bet he got the trash bag from one of the other events that night. Jason wore black and might have fit in with the service crews at the events. Del would have had his security uniform on and would also have looked like he was supposed to be there. If the killer had to ditch the knife, all he had to do was sneak into a different party and steal a trash bag. The idea of getting someone else to ditch it on their curb strikes me as particularly genius."

"Evil genius, anyway. I wonder what the police know."

"You're going to have to develop a network of official connections in the future, Janey. We can't do every case in the dark like this."

"You're right…but at the moment, I have no idea how to do that."

The office phone rang. Jake answered it and started talking restaurant business stuff. Jane waved and left.

She didn't want to go home and face Gemma just yet, so she went to the convention center to try and find Lafayette.

At the convention center, Jane went straight to the information booth. The assistant manning the station walkied Lafayette for Jane.

When Lafayette arrived, she led Jane to a small office like you might see at a car dealership, just a little room with a desk and some chairs. "What can I do for you?" Lafayette was petite, but she had an intimidating presence. Lines around her mouth seemed to indicate a permanent frown.

"Thanks for making time for me." Jane took a seat, but maintained her posture. "Jake Crawford hired me to look into the murder of Michelle Smith. I've been in touch with one of your security guards, Beth, and she told me an interesting story."

Lafayette took a seat. Her face relaxed. "Did she?"

"Apparently Beth's boyfriend, Del, got himself administrative leave because of his actions the night of the murder." Jane raised one eyebrow and smiled. "But he tried to hide that from his girlfriend."

Lafayette chuckled. "And you met him here not long after, pretending like he hadn't gotten into trouble."

"That's right." Jane began to drum her pencil on her notepad, but stopped herself. She didn't want to appear either nervous or impatient.

"And you want to know what he did to get himself in trouble."

"Beth told me a version of the story."

"But you wonder if Del can be trusted?" Lafayette looked at her watch. "He's a good guy. He has a past, but he's a good guy. Why he snuck off with so much going on in the center that night is only as mysterious as why the other guy was late. It was poor planning. Del's not the brightest bulb, but he's not bad." She nodded in a way that appeared conclusive.

"So what became of the bag of trash?"

"Ahh." Lafayette folded her hands. "The police questioned janitorial. They didn't see the bag in the bathroom stall. The current theory is that the killer noticed where Del put it and went back for it."

"That makes sense, however, that bag of trash is the proof that what Del said was true."

Lafayette sighed. She leaned forward. "Crawford hired you to look into the murder, which is...odd. Nonetheless, you are here. The police have been here already and asked all of these questions. I have a feeling you will 'solve' this murder when you read whodunit on Twitter."

Jane frowned. "You feel I am asking the wrong questions."

"And the wrong person."

Jane rubbed her lips together. It seemed to her that Lafayette knew something, and instead of being the wrong questions to the wrong person, Jane was onto it, and that made the head of security nervous. Jane crossed her legs and settled back into her chair. "Why were there only two men scheduled to be in the security office that night?"

Lafayette lifted her eyebrow. "One called in sick and one was late. I called around, but two was the best we could do."

"Who called in sick?" Jane toyed with her pencil, hoping it made her look nonchalant.

"One of our new guards."

"Is he in today?"

"No." Lafayette looked from her watch to the door and then to her watch again. She eventually settled her eyes on Jane and stood up. "Good luck with your investigation."

"Just one more question." Jane scrambled for a question that would make Lafayette sit down and keep talking. Lafayette didn't like the direction her questions had gone…the bag of trash was a problem, or proving what Del claimed was a problem. Which was it? "What other evidence do you have to prove what Del claimed is true? Oh, and what's Del's last name?"

Lafayette inhaled sharply. "Del's last name? It's Willis. Surveillance video clearly shows him entering the bathroom, followed by a man with a hat who kept his face pointedly away from the cameras. The man was carrying a big, black trash bag."

Lafayette walked out.

Del Willis.

Since the office was empty, Jane made herself comfortable. She preferred her laptop for lengthy trawls through Google, but she had her phone, and a notebook, so she could learn something before she had to go again. But before she got any further than laying everything out on the table, she remembered something Beth had said. Meryl Lafayette had a son in the police. What if the police had come down, chatted up staff, learned that Del was a Willis, and then Meryl Lafayette had had a conversation with her son that tied Del Willis to Rose of Sharon Willis, the nice, kindly, nonviolent protester who happened to have a son—with a criminal record?

CHAPTER 16

OSWEGO VALLEY MEMORIAL GARDENS had fit Michelle Smith's funeral in on New Year's Eve Day to accommodate the next of kin—Michelle's son Doug's—travel schedule.

Jane shivered in her black raincoat. The wind whipped her hair and the rain fell in freezing sheets. She hung to the back of the crowd of grievers as they made their way to the graveside. The frosted grass crunched under her feet. The roads would be dangerous after the freezing rain, but Jane tried not to worry about it.

Michelle's mortal remains were being buried, and a hundred or so of her friends, old church members, and families from her school had gathered to say goodbye. Carrie, the assistant Jane had met a couple of days ago, wept into the end of her brown plaid scarf. Sasha Henry held a white handkerchief to her nose, and her eyes were painfully red. Michelle Smith's son Doug choked up during his speech. He couldn't finish what he had to say about his mom, who had just retired to see her grandkids grow up.

Jane squeezed Jake's hand. New Year's Eve Day promised treacherous driving for the night, and the tangible grief in the crowd made it obvious none of those present would be ringing in the New Year with good cheer. Jane wanted nothing more than to get back inside—and take some pictures of the guest book.

With a crowd almost as big as the one at the charity event, she and Jake had their work cut out for them, if they really intended to check each name against the other list. Jane took a deep, strengthening breath. It was the most detectivey thing she could think of, and she had to start doing some real detective work. She couldn't let this murder get solved by chance, or worse yet, by the regular police.

"They're praying," Jake whispered.

Jane bowed her head.

From the back of the crowd they could sneak back into the funeral home before everyone else—but only by a minute or two.

The pastor of Michelle's old church finished the prayer and began a song. It was thirty degrees, wet, and December thirty-first, but the crowd sang about dancing on streets that were golden. Jane gave Jake's hand a little tug, ready to turn back, but Jake just pulled her arm closer as he sang.

When the last lines of the last time through the bridge died down, a new song rose up, but this time from the back. Gruff but emotional voices, quiet at first, but growing stronger, started in on "Apples and Bananas."

Jane swung around. Forty or more Helpers, with Rose of Sharon in the middle, held hands in a semicircle, almost like an embrace around the mourners. Their faces turned up to the steely, cold sky, their cheeks tearstained. They sang the silly camp song almost reverently, then stopped.

Jane recognized Yuri at the tail end of the crowd, shuffling his feet. Yuri had come…to make it clear he wasn't the murderer? He had hung around towards the unlikely end of her suspects list for a long time…his appearance at the funeral shot him up a few notches.

She'd have to watch him a little closer.

"May I say a few words?" Rose of Sharon's voice cracked, and she was hard to hear, even from where Jane stood. The pastor didn't hear her at all and dismissed the crowd, asking them to return to the reception inside.

Jane led the crowd inside, passing a confused and distraught-looking Rose of Sharon as she went.

Jane stopped in the foyer and watched the mourners go into the reception. Many peeled away and went to the parking lot instead, but a solid fifty or more stayed for the potluck. As she expected, they grouped together around tables and didn't intermingle. "Could you go in and sort of meet people?" Jane nodded towards the door. "Maybe go table to table finding out who all is staying."

"Sure." Jake focused on a loud table near the front. "I'll case the joint while you take pictures of the guest book."

They parted, but Jane still hung back. The Helpers were lined up to sign the guest book. Jane spotted Valeria with her husband and, almost too good to be true, she saw Del and Beth with Rose of Sharon and two other girls…perhaps the daughters Clove and Isis.

Rose of Sharon had said that her girls went to Trillium Montessori. They looked to be teenagers, so perhaps they were a second family of sorts. Much younger than Del, the thirty-two-year-old security guard.

Jane stepped quietly across the deep rug and joined the Willis group. "I'm glad you all were able to make it." She kept her voice low.

Rose of Sharon gave her a side hug. "We tried to be on time, but it was difficult on the bridge today."

"I'm hungry." The shorter of the two girls sounded like a child, though she was clearly in her late teen years. Her eyes didn't seem to focus well, and she sort of slumped against Del's arm.

"Shush. We'll eat in a minute." Del patted her arm in a brotherly fashion. Beth stood with the other Willis girl, who was taller and had an appealing look of curiosity on her face.

"Let's say hello to Doug, and then we can leave." Rose of Sharon took the hungry girl's arm from Del and went into the reception.

Jane tapped Beth's shoulder. "Do you think Del told Rose of Sharon about our event so she could protest it?"

Beth frowned. "He loves his stepmom to death, but he has never been a protester. Not even after Isis's accident." Beth hurried after her boyfriend.

Jane kept up with her. "What accident?"

Beth checked out where Rose of Sharon was in the room and then stopped. "She's got a peanut allergy and almost died from it. When she came home, they realized she had permanent brain damage."

"Oh my gosh! That's awful!" Jane swallowed.

"Del was devastated. He loves his baby sisters like they're his own. He was really angry about it for a long time, but he thought Rose of Sharon dealt with it wrong."

"What did Del think she should have done?"

Beth chewed on her bottom lip.

"You can tell me."

Beth shook her head.

"It's okay. You don't have to."

Over Beth's shoulder, Jane saw Rose of Sharon embrace Doug Smith. Doug held onto her in a tight embrace, his head rested on her shoulder.

"Michelle was a very, very good friend of Rose's, wasn't she?"

"Yes." Beth paused. "Del thought…well, I mean, he doesn't think it anymore, but at the time, he was young—just seventeen—and he thought his dad should have sued the school. Everyone knew about Isis's allergies."

Jane's heart was beating a mile a minute. Miter might have owed Smith a lot of money, but this Del kid had a serious, long-term grudge against Michelle Smith. And he had been out of his office during the murder and had gotten rid of the murder weapon.

Jane scanned the room for Jake. He had his arm around a grey-haired woman who was laughing, even though tears rolled down her cheeks.

"They did a craft with peanut shells. It was too much for her and she went into anaphylactic shock. By the time she was revived at the hospital, she had been without oxygen for too long."

"How could Rose of Sharon find it in her heart to forgive Michelle for this?"

"How does anyone forgive? Rose of Sharon loves Jesus. Plus, Michelle was at a conference that week. She couldn't have stopped the tragedy. Rose of Sharon understands that. And of course, Del gets it now. But back then, he was deeply angry."

"Please, if you could just answer one more question…why does Del have a criminal record?"

"It's not what you're thinking, don't worry. He just smuggled a lot of weed in from Canada. It wasn't a violent crime." Beth gave Jane's arm a squeeze and then joined Rose of Sharon.

Jane made her way to Jake, one eye on Del.

At the family table, Doug grasped Del's hand in a two-fisted shake and pulled him in for a hug. Did Doug have any clue that Del had just murdered his mother?

Jane dragged Jake away from his hobnobbing and found a quiet spot in the corner of the foyer. She relayed everything she had learned from Beth and then took a deep breath. "Well? What do you think?"

"If that had happened to Phoebe, I'd be mad too."

"Should we watch him, though? What if he tries something here? Maybe to the teacher in charge that day or something?"

"I'd be mad, Jane, but then I'd grow up, like Del did. And I wouldn't kill someone." Jake put his arm around Jane's waist. "But great detective skills."

"I think Del just became the number one suspect in a major way. No one-hundred-thousand-dollar judgment could compare with a sister who was permanently disabled." Jane shivered.

"You can say that because you've never owed anyone one hundred thousand dollars."

"If money was such a problem, how could he leave such a big donation at the event?"

"Maybe his money problems are over." Jake had an eye on the reception hall while they talked.

"Then why kill Michelle? I don't think Jason Miter did it." Jane chewed her lip.

"Any other reasonable suspects?"

"Do you know anything about Yuri Bean?"

"Is that a hipster band?"

"Nope, he's a Helper I met at the event. His wife was a nervous wreck and he acted very suspiciously. Plus, he's here at the funeral." Jane tried to spot him the crowd but couldn't.

"Do you have a motive for him?"

"Not yet."

Jake shrugged. "Then let's get back in there and get chatting. I've learned more about Lake Oswego's Montessori school set than I ever guessed there was to know."

"Did you learn anything to the point?"

"I learned that the table just behind the door there is shocked that Jason Miter and his wife would dare show up at this funeral. If I were you, I'd avoid that table. Once they get started, they don't stop." Jake directed Jane to an almost empty table in the back. "And I learned from Tammy Miter, Jason's wife, that they are appealing the judgment. She said that they have paid all of their back bills now—sold some property at the beach to do it—and she's hoping to get the rest of the fees tossed out, especially as the plaintiff is dead."

"Whoa."

"Exactly. Owing a person a lot of money seems like a possible motive. But if you throw in the death as a reason to get the judgment reversed, you go from could-be to really hot motive."

Though they whispered, the man in the brown suit sitting on the other side of the long rectangle lifted his eyebrow. "Think you know who did it?"

Jane blushed.

Jake smiled. "Maybe."

"So do I." The stranger moved to a closer chair. "See that woman over there?" He pointed at a short, round blonde woman.

"That's Tammy Miter," Jake said.

"Keep an eye on her. She's acting very guilty."

"And who are you?" Jane whispered.

"Detective Benedict." He offered his hand. "I hate to say it, since you're both so young, and seem to not understand how far whispers carry, but you have done a pretty good job in a very short time."

Jane grinned.

"Can I see your ID?" Jake asked.

Detective Benedict pulled out his wallet and showed his police ID.

"Were you teasing us about Tammy Miter?" Jane scrunched her mouth.

"I might have been. But I have to say, you guys have made a lot of valid points throughout the whole funeral. It has been worth it to me to shadow you."

Jane scratched her head. "So, I'm a criminal justice student at Portland State, and I'm planning on going into private detection. What do I do now? I mean, if I have a strong theory and decent evidence, what am I supposed to do with it?"

"A private investigator, eh? You put it in a manila envelope and exchange it for a check in a dark alley."

Jane inhaled sharply. "Not like that. More like a…consulting detective."

"Like Sherlock, huh? That's a good show."

Jake shook his head, subtly. The detective was mostly making fun of them, but Jane wasn't going to waste the opportunity. "Listen, I just want to know what's the best way of getting any information to the police. Is there a certain office that likes to take tips? A particular rank of cop I should ask for? I don't want to do this wrong."

Detective Benedict smiled, but just with his lips. "If it's a case we are actively working on, you're already doing it wrong. But feel free to call the main phone line and pass off any info you gather." He left the table, hands in his pockets. Smug.

"He's not going to be my insider, I guess." Jane rested her chin on her hands.

"Guess not."

"And I guess I need some proper evidence before I call in with a tip, since Detective Benedict all but said he had listened in to both of our theories." Jane scanned the room again for Yuri Bean. "We don't have any advantage over the police now."

"Never did."

"Probably true. But we need to get the advantage, so let's see if we can bring the crisis to a head."

"Like bait the suspects into a confession?"

"Got a better idea?"

"Nope." Jake stood up. "Who first?"

The Willis clan were seated with a dozen slightly threatening-looking protester types. The Miters—just Jason and Tammy—were alone. "Let's go thank Mr. and Mrs. Miter for their generous donation, yes?" Jane took Jake's arm.

"Sounds good to me."

CHAPTER 17

JAKE KEPT A PROTECTIVE ARM AROUND JANE'S WAIST as they walked to the table where the Miters sat, alone.

"Hey Jason, this is my wife, Jane. Tell her Trillium will be fine."

Jason extended his hand. "Nice to meet you."

Jane squared her shoulders. It was a cover story; that made it okay to lie, right? "Thanks."

"Jake was telling us that your daughter will start at Trillium next year."

Jane did her best to keep a straight face. "I'm just not so sure anymore."

Jake squeezed. "Babe, you had Tulip on the waiting list for a year. You've got to let her go now."

"*Tulip,*" Jane said, barely stifling a gag, "could always go to the preschool at Prez Elementary, where we went."

"Trillium is a great school. It's worth every sacrifice." Tammy sniffled into a tissue. "I just can't believe she's gone."

"But will it be the same without Michelle? I mean, I know she didn't live here anymore, but she still had an influence…she was still *alive.*" Jane choked up a little. Tammy's grief seemed so real.

"I just wish we could have resolved our legal issues before she passed." Jason's voice was gravelly, as though he barely had his emotions in control.

"I think she understood our dilemma though, honey." Tammy patted her husband's arm. "She did what she had to do, and we understood." Tammy's eyes welled up again.

They seemed sad, and maybe in la-la land about how much the director of the school they habitually shafted really *understood* their situation, but they didn't seem…guilty.

"It is an expensive school." Jane used a wistful tone. "Part of me thinks it would be wiser to bank the money for college and just homeschool Tulip."

"We've talked about this before, Janey," Jake said. "We don't want to have one of those weird homeschooled kids."

Tammy laughed. "My kids aren't weird."

"Don't listen to him, Tammy," Jane said with a smile. "His ex-wife homeschools, and he's really mad about it."

Jason frowned.

"Er…they aren't his kids." Jane looked at Jake helplessly. As newlyweds with a preschooler they were just barely believable…as a second marriage…

"Still a little bitter about being jilted." Jake chuckled. "And for such an old guy too…" He laughed in a knowing kind of way, and Jason relaxed. Jake had such an easygoing manner with his lies…just enough detail to make it sound like he had said his ex-wife left him for an old rich guy with kids, but not so many details that it sounded like a lie. He was kind of the master of the cover story.

"If it's between Trillium and homeschooling," Tammy said, "I'd recommend homeschooling all the way. I don't regret one minute I've spent teaching my kids."

Jane nodded slowly. "I'm really leaning that way."

"You should call me. We can get together for coffee or something. I love helping moms start out." Tammy pulled a phone from her purse.

So far they had failed to make the Miters even hint at guilt, much less confess all. Jane tried to turn her head and find Del, but Tammy was asking for the number.

Jane accepted her phone and typed in a number that was just a digit off. She smiled. "Thanks."

The room was thinning now, and the table full of protesters was empty.

They crunched their way across the frosty gravel to the Jag Jake had inherited when his parents died. "If it wasn't the Miters, it just had to be Del. But how can we prove it now?" Jane clicked her seat buckle.

"You're going to have to pray hard about it." Jake pulled into the almost-stopped traffic. "You're really leaning towards being a homeschooling detective-missionary?"

"You'd name our only daughter *Tulip*?"

Jane spent the rest of the afternoon drumming her fingers, praying for inspiration, and getting ready for Jake's family New Year's Eve party.

Gemma lurked silently in the living room while Jane ran around looking for her earrings. She moped on the couch while Jane tried desperately to put curls in her stick-straight hair.

Gemma perched on the edge of the bathtub while Jane attempted to create subtle cat's eyes with her new liquid liner.

"We're going to have to come to some kind of new housing arrangement."

"What?" Jane turned her head, smearing the liner.

"I can't live with you if you're with Jake."

"But I'm not really with Jake." Jane sucked in a sharp breath. Yes, she was. She was absolutely with Jake now. And probably had been, in her heart, for quite a while.

"Spare me."

"It's not like we're dating, Gemma." Which was true. Because kissing and canoodling wasn't exactly the same thing as dating.

"Because it's been two days since you jumped him at the party. You haven't had time to go on a date yet."

Gemma had a point. Jane's heart sank. "Are you asking me to move out?"

Gemma shrugged. "You and I—we're more than just friends, aren't we?"

"We're family." Jane wiped the black liner off of her face. She looked better natural, anyway.

"But we've always been good friends, too."

"Of course." Jane spritzed herself with a little White Musk—the only scent she had. Gemma would get over her funk. She had to. It wasn't like she had stolen Jake from her or anything. This Jake thing was fate. Predestination. It couldn't have been avoided.

"Well, you broke the code. Friends don't go after each other's men."

Jane gritted her teeth. "Oh, grow up." She stopped. She hadn't meant to say that out loud.

"Excuse me?"

Jane squared her shoulders, yet another of her constant attempts to appear more confident than she felt. "He tried to let you know nicely that he wasn't interested. He really did."

"That still doesn't make it right for you to go after him."

"I never went after him, I swear. I avoided him. I ignored him. I did everything I could to avoid falling for him."

"You played games with him, then."

Jane put her lipstick down. "I didn't."

"Rent is due next week. After that, move out." Gemma walked out without a backwards glance.

Last time she had found herself homeless, she had moved into Jake's family home. This time, that didn't seem like the wisest idea.

Jake's family party was larger than Jane expected. The party was upstairs at the old family house in Laurelhurst—in the ballroom she hadn't seen since the funeral for Jake's parents. Jake seemed to have cousins, and friends of cousins, spilling out of every corner.

The only person Jane recognized was Phoebe. Rather than cling to Phoebe, or Jake, who seemed to be in a place of complete Zen as party host, she hung back, in what had once been a small card room, googling the Willis family.

She couldn't find anything about Isis's peanut allergy incident on old news sites or on allergy blogs. She did learn that permanent brain damage was a rare, but real, potential risk of an anaphylactic shock reaction to anything, including peanuts.

Poor Isis.

And poor Rose of Sharon as well.

But what about Del? How protective had Isis's much-older brother been?

The DJ switched from Frank Sinatra to Bruno Mars. The lights went down and the disco ball flashed bright snowflakes of light around the ballroom. Midnight was near.

Jake peeked around the door frame. "Put away the case for one song, Jane."

He always made her smile. Even before the other party. She hadn't told him about the homelessness situation yet. Her heart fluttered in her chest just to look at him. She pushed the phone aside. "Sure. Why not."

"Come dance, it's our song." He took her by the hand and led her to the center of the action.

Jake could dance.

He spun her and turned her and dipped her until she was dizzy. "Our song?" She was breathless, but managed to ask as he pulled her against his chest.

"I think I wanna marry you," Jake sang along as he spun her again.

She closed her eyes, but all she saw was the other ring. It was too soon—way too soon—for talking like this.

He pulled her back in and wrapped both arms around her. "I know what you're thinking. Every time I look at you, I know what you're thinking, but it's our song. You know it is. I've been planning on marrying you for a long time now."

"Maybe I need more dancing juice?"

Jake kissed her. "No. Not you. All you need is a little more time."

She felt completely sheltered in his arms, even though he moved too fast—around the dance floor, in life, whatever. His lips never seemed to leave her neck, her cheek, her lips, but his touch was light, a hint of a kiss, a nuzzle, almost imperceptible. He turned with her, slowly around the room, and then stood still.

She was close enough to whisper anything, and no one else in the crowded room would know what she said. "Gemma kicked me out."

"Guilting me into a rush wedding won't work. You deserve the real deal." Jake grinned.

"That's not what I meant." She swatted his bottom.

"That's just going to make me say it again."

"Never mind."

The song changed, and Jane rested her head on his shoulder. He swayed in place like it was a junior high dance.

"I will never let you be homeless, you know that, right?"

"Mmm." His words were nice, and she believed him. But of course she wouldn't take a hand out.

"I've got a lot of restaurants you could clean for rent money." He nibbled her ear.

"It's time to count down!" the DJ hollered.

"Ten!" the whole crowd shouted in one voice.

She counted in her head. The New Year did not look anything like she pictured. By the count of five, Jake had managed to ease her to the back of the crowd, a darker, more private corner.

"Listen, Jane, I know you don't take help, but whatever. That's lame, by the way. Anything you need, okay? Whatever I have is yours. And…if you wanted to—"

"One!"

Jane didn't want to hear him propose, so she put both of her hands on his face and kissed him like they were playing sardines again.

He picked her up, and she wrapped her legs around his waist.

Without stopping for a breath, he carried her to the card room where he had found her.

He dropped her on the table and stepped away. "Phew." He panted. "No more of that, all right?"

Jane was hot. She knew her face was red. Her heart beat so hard it made her rib cage shake. "Yeah. Yes. You're right."

"I'm right."

"Yes. Of course."

"Yeah. I am."

"Of course. No more of that."

"Right." He stepped closer, and rested his fingertips on the table she sat on.

"Nope."

"Exactly."

"Because."

"Of course. Exactly." He leaned down and kissed her again.

"Crap."

"Exactly." Jake smiled, and exhaled slowly. "Yeah, I've got to…do something else now." He left.

Jane buried her head in her hands. This was going to be a problem.

Jane bunked in her old room that night. The Crawfords hadn't had live-in help—a real live-in maid—for at least a generation, but they kept the little staff bedrooms furnished for extra guest beds.

She had a feeling that Jake knew she was there. She was only a little disappointed that he didn't come visit—because, really.

That would have been a problem.

Despite not having any of the "dancing juice" she suspected had been available last night, she had a headache. Gemma's roommate-drama tantrum wasn't going to be a long-term problem. Gemma would get over it as soon as she needed Jane to front her a month's rent. But the situation with

Del…getting away with murder…that had weighed on her for most of the few hours she spent in bed.

Their idea at the funeral had been to goad him into a confession. Right now, he was weak. He had been taken off work, had had a little trouble with his girlfriend, and had a murder on his chest. She was sure she could get him to confess, but she would love Jake's help with it.

Which begged the question: did Jake really have time to be her partner in the detective business? His job running the family restaurant business had been all-consuming over the summer and fall. She chalked his recent spate of free time up to bad winter sales and the holidays. But when things got back to normal, would he have time to play Nick and Nora with her? And was it selfish of her to hope he would?

Yes. Of course it was. She didn't want to change her life plans for Isaac. Why should Jake have to adopt her dream?

Fortunately, today was a holiday, and Jake was the boss. If he wanted to, he could probably take the day off to hunt down a killer.

Jane pulled her hair into a ponytail. She was glad she wore leggings with her miniskirt last night, but wished she had realized she was going to spend the night and had packed a toothbrush. Feeling more than a little scuzzy, she went downstairs for breakfast.

"Mi vida." Jake sat at the breakfast bar, dark shadows under his eyes. His voice was hoarse and his hair stood on end. He yawned. "What are you making for breakfast?"

Jane looked at her watch. "A quick getaway. I'm so sorry."

"Where are you taking me?"

"I have two post–New Year's Eve houses to clean today." Jane took a deep breath. She'd have to run home and face Gemma, since real life didn't stop for pouting cousins.

Jake rested his head in his hand and closed his eyes with a smile. "Hard work is cute."

"When I'm done, I'll call you."

"That's nice." Jake laid his head on the table. "I hate mornings."

"It's nine." Jane kind of wanted to sit on his lap, but refrained. She was going to have to learn to keep it together if she wanted to have half a chance at a nice, long courtship.

"Exactly." He stretched his arms over his head. "Are you sure you have to go?"

"Even if I had won the lottery last night instead of getting kicked out of my apartment, I would need to go. I made a commitment."

Jake grinned. "You did win the lottery last night. And if you don't call me by noon, I'm coming to find you. Do you understand?"

With an act of self-control that surprised her, Jane did not leap into his arms. "Yessir." She scrambled out of his house as fast as she could, only hoping the neighbors weren't asking what that nice Adler girl had been doing at Jake's house all night. When she turned to look one more time, she noticed that the driveway was still full of cars.

They hadn't been even remotely alone.

She stared at the cars. They hadn't been alone, but she had thought of nothing but…*that* since he kissed her at the other party.

This was not how God wanted her to fall in love. This was not okay. She sat on the curb and shivered. So much for being ready for the mission field. She was no better than an adolescent kid.

Perhaps that was what her parents, and teachers, and everyone else had been talking about when she tried so hard to run away with the missionaries the year before. Perhaps…she wasn't as grown-up as she thought.

She took five minutes to pray, heartfelt and contrite. Whatever path God had for her, it had to include a lot of growing up if she was ever going to be the woman she had thought she was.

She had an hour before she needed to get to her first house, so when she noticed something familiar about one of the cars in the driveway, she didn't mind taking a minute to check it out.

It was just a series of bumper stickers, that was all. One that said "HLP." One that said "I like to eat" and had a picture of an apple and a banana on it. A stick figure family with a dad, mom, and two girl figures, each with long hippy braids. Another sticker that said "Vegan Pride."

Had a Helper come to Jake's family party? And if so…would that person know anything about Del's relationship with his sisters?

Jane leaned casually against the car, hoping no one would know she was looking inside. She fiddled with the door handle, not really expecting it to pop open, but it did.

She crawled inside and popped open the jockey box. The registration was right on top.

Del Willis.

Jane shot out of the car and ran back into the house. She slid into the kitchen and caught herself on the breakfast bar.

"He's still here, then?"

Jane nodded. She needed to catch her breath before she could start on her questions.

"Before you yell, remember my head."

"I won't yell—he could hear."

"Ah, my only saving grace." Jake passed Jane a cup of coffee. "I had hoped you'd come back."

"What's he doing here?" Jane kept her voice at a whisper.

"I invited everyone I could think of and had them pass the word along. You didn't really think I was related to all of those people, did you?"

"But why didn't you tell me?"

Jake held his finger to his lips, though she hadn't raised her voice. "To be completely honest, it was because every time I looked at you, all I could think about was how much I wanted to kiss you. It was New Year's Eve. I planned on making a citizen's arrest. But every time you walked past, or I walked past you, since you stayed cooped up in that card room most of the night, I forgot."

"Well, what do we do now?"

"We find him. I assume he's not the only one still here?"

"No, there are five other cars out there, too."

"The let's keep this chill, okay? Let's just go around the house looking for guests and asking them if they want to stay for breakfast." He took her hand and kissed it.

They went upstairs first, knowing that a mixed crowd of random invites from the grapevine had likely ended up in bedrooms. Phoebe was in her own room with four girlfriends all getting dressed. Jake covered his eyes. "Breakfast orders?"

"You can't cook. We're going out." Phoebe tossed a pillow at her brother. "And shut the door."

The next bedroom had been slept in, but was empty. On their way to the third, Del came padding down the hall in yesterday's clothes.

"Breakfast order?" Jake squeezed Jane's hand.

"Ah, no thanks." Del raked his hand through his hair. "I've got to run. Beth is meeting me at her mom's house."

"Before you go..." Jane smiled. "Did you guys have fun last night?"

Jake snorted, but quietly.

"Sure." Del pulled his phone out and checked the time.

"It was the second-best party of the year, in my opinion." Jane was doing her best to drag the conversation out. Del couldn't leave yet.

"Yeah. It was fun." Del eyed the open bedroom door.

Jake pulled Jane to the next room. "Keep it chill."

"Good morning—" Jane stopped.

Aunt Marjory sat on the bed.

"I see you stayed over, yet again." Marjory pinned her hair back. "Quite a 'little' family party last night, Jake."

"Well, you know how these things are, Aunty. That Pheebs of yours is quite a social butterfly."

"Ahh. Sure, she is."

"And, um, I didn't stay the night with Jake, just so you know. Really. I was upstairs the whole time."

"Shhh," Jake whispered.

"Alone." She let go of his hand.

Marjory raised an eyebrow. "You don't have to justify yourselves to me. I'm not in charge here." She stood up and cleared her throat. Jake stepped aside.

"I won't be staying for breakfast." Aunt Marjory left.

"Why didn't you tell her?" Jane searched Jake's face. A rosy shade of embarrassed spread across his cheeks.

"I had invited a killer to the house, you know."

"And?"

"And I couldn't leave you up there by yourself when I knew for certain everyone else who stayed would be staying in one of the many nice bedrooms on this level."

"So?"

"So I stayed up all night by your door. When I heard you get up, I left. But…Marjory saw me coming away from your room this morning. She said she was assessing the damage."

"Ahh." Jane gritted her teeth. Jake was destined to ruin her good name. Innocently, of course, but that wouldn't matter to people who liked gossip.

"The point to remember is that Del Willis did not sneak into your bedroom last night and stick a knife in you."

"What?" The voice behind them was deep, shocked, and belonged to Del.

"Oh, ah, ha ha." Jake tried to laugh.

Jane tried to smile.

"I didn't hear that right, did I?"

"He was attempting to be my knight in armor, I guess." Jane managed another nervous laugh.

"But…" Del looked confused. "Why would you think I—?" His face began to show recognition. "Because of the bag of trash. Someone told you about that." His face blanched.

"It doesn't look good, bro. Between that and your sister." Jake shrugged.

"We would understand why you had a grudge for so long," Jane added.

"A grudge? Against who? Michelle?" Del took a step back.

"Because of Isis," Jane said.

Del took off down the stairs. He hesitated at the bottom.

Jane was frozen in her spot. Was he scared or guilt ridden?

Jake was almost to him when he turned and ran towards the back door.

Jane took the steps two at a time and caught up with both boys outside.

"Is that why you invited me here? Because you thought I killed Michelle Smith?"

Jane and Jake stood silently, Jane behind his car, and Jake between Del and Del's only way out.

Del held his hands up. "You can't pin this on me."

Was that a confession? Jane's phone shook in her hand. She wanted to call the police this second, but…was it a confession? She fished around in her other pocket and found the card for the snotty Detective Benedict. She kept silent, and so did Jake.

Del was pinned between the other cars and Jake. Jane counted on him not driving away while she stood at the back of his car. He pulled open the car door anyway, but then just stood there, shaking. "You cannot pin this on me. I didn't touch that woman."

"How did you know she was going to be there?" Jane asked.

"I didn't know anything."

"Did you see her on the security camera and decide to get her while you could? Your one shot while she was in town?" Jake added.

"Or…" Jane went slowly, the idea forming while she spoke. "Did you see she was there on the security camera and call your mommy to come? And then *she* did it?"

Del spit.

"It wasn't his mom, remember, Jane? It was a man in black."

"Jason Miter?"

"Why not? Did you see Michelle at the party and call Jason? You know him because his kids went to school with your sisters? Something like that? You knew about his money troubles because this is just a big small town and gossip spreads?" Jane was on a roll. "No! You knew about his troubles because his son Ethan, who we guessed was fifteen and definitely went to school with your sisters, talks too much."

Del gripped the door.

"I'm going to make a guess," Jake said. "If I'm right, panic, okay? I think Ethan keeps in touch with Clove, and you heard from Clove that her parents were really, really upset with Michelle, right?"

Del's jaw flexed, and sweat popped out on his forehead.

"So, you were sitting in your little office, and you saw Michelle waltz into the party." Jake leaned templed his fingers and lifted an eyebrow. "Then you called the senior Mr. Miter, Jason, to come take care of a mutual problem." While Jake spoke, Jane dialed Detective Benedict's number.

"I didn't call anyone." Del stood up straight, an almost cocky look in his eye. "You can check the phone records. And the cameras. I didn't call anyone that night."

"Of course not." Jane smirked. She had her finger on this one. "Because your stepmom is still friends with Michelle. Michelle told *her* about the party, which is how the Helpers ended up there to protest, and how you knew in advance that Michelle would be there." Jane smiled at Jake, who gave her a thumbs-up.

Del dove into his car and slammed the door shut. He hit the locks and started the engine.

Detective Benedict answered. Jane tossed the phone to Jake and lay across the back of Del's car.

Nonviolent protest was a language Del spoke.

"Hey there, buddy," Jake said. "We just solved your murder. If you want to know what we know, you might want to get here." There was a lengthy silence from Jake, but Del revved his engine.

Adrenaline pumped through Jane, tinged with a touch of mind-rattling fear, but mostly she just wanted to win. Del could not leave before the police got here.

"Nope, we've got the killer right here. Do we have to? Are you absolutely sure?" Jake didn't hide the disgust in his voice. Then, "Let him go, Jane. We aren't allowed to keep him here."

Jane stood up. "Really? We have to let him go?"

Jake rolled his eyes. "No evidence, yo."

Del backed out of the driveway as soon as Jane had stepped to the side.

"But we caught him."

Jake shrugged. "We'll be there in ten minutes." He hung up.

"What now?" Jane kicked a rock.

"Now we go to Detective Benedict and tell him everything we know. We tell him how Del reacted to our story. And we let the cops arrest them."

"Why can't we do it?"

Jake draped his arm over her shoulder. "Because we're private investigators, not cops. But I think we did good, and I don't think they'll get away with it."

Jake hadn't given Jane enough time to get changed, so they met the detective at his office in last night's party clothes. They laid the whole story out for him.

"But you don't have any evidence. Any proof that what you are saying is true." Detective Benedict could only have had a deeper frown if he had had a big, droopy mustache.

"You could check and see if the Miters were telling the truth about paying off their debt," Jane said.

"I'll ask the charity to try and cash the donation tomorrow," Jake said.

Benedict shrugged. "Murders take a long time to solve, kids. This one is only a week old."

"But that doesn't mean Jason Miter and Del Willis didn't do it." Jane's voice trembled. She'd have to figure out a better way to fake strength. Or…she'd have to practice relying on God to be her strength. That idea alone calmed her down. "And some murders are solved very quickly. When you know who did it, but don't have evidence, what do you do next?"

Detective Benedict smiled, just a little, but his eyes were still hooded. "We start asking a lot more questions, and we do it at the station." Detective Benedict stood up. "And now, I have a few questions to ask Del Willis about this conversation he just had with you." He paused. "Too bad that stepmom of his is so good at working the system."

He escorted them outside. "Thanks for the tip. You might, just might, not be the worst investigator in the world. But if I were you, I'd steer clear of murder from now on."

Back in the car, Jane exhaled slowly. "I am so disappointed."

"Don't be. You did great. Totally earned your keep."

"Do you think Benedict believed it?"

"More to the point, Del believes we know everything. So, if you don't mind, I think I'll just hang out with you while you clean, yes?"

Jane nodded. She was too confused to speak. She might not be a bad investigator. This was the first time anyone but Jake had suggested this could be the case.

They had the radio on while they cleaned both houses, listening for any news. But the only thing Jane learned was that Jake wasn't completely useless at mopping.

"You didn't think my dad would let me work for him if I didn't start at the bottom, did you?"

Jane laughed. Jake was so comfortable. He just…fit. Didn't ask her to change, didn't expect her to be someone she wasn't. She couldn't help but compare him to…well. It wasn't fair, really. Isaac wasn't meant to be, so he'd never compare well.

18

"GEMMA, JUST SIT AND LISTEN, OKAY?" Jane asked.

Gemma looked from Jane to Jake. Her face turned beet red.

"Don't be embarrassed. It's my fault." Jane sat on the floor. "I totally introduced you to him so that he would fall in love with you and leave me alone."

"Ahem, I'm in the room with you."

"No, you're in the kitchen making dinner." Jane tried to keep a straight face.

"Yes, ma'am."

"You were going to marry Isaac Daniels, so even if it was obvious that Jake was into you, you'd be gone eventually, and Jake and I would be great buds. It would have worked out." Gemma's voice was quiet. Her big, brown eyes were wet with tears.

"No, it wouldn't have," Jake piped in from the kitchen.

"Jake—quiet."

Jake turned the radio up.

Jane took a deep breath. “I am seriously sorry that I created this embarrassing, hopeless situation. But please don’t kick me out of the apartment. I don’t know where I would go.”

“You could go to Arizona.”

“If they don’t catch Del and Jason fast, I’ll send you there myself,” Jake said.

“I’m not going to Arizona, Gemma. I’m staying here, and you are forgiving me and wishing me happiness, okay?”

Gemma let out a slow breath. “It is such a bad idea to jump from relationship to relationship like this. How well do you know this guy?” Her face was still sad, but a twinkle in her eye said she was willing to try.

“I’ve only known him since I was fourteen, so I can see why you are concerned.”

“You girls don’t have anything to eat. How do you live?”

“We tend to order takeout from this nice guy we know…” Gemma said. Her voice broke, but she laughed.

“You are totally the second-best girl in the world, Gem. Er, third.” Jake shrugged apologetically. “I do have a sister.”

Gemma wiped her eyes with the back of her hand and laughed. “I don’t think I’m ready to be happy third wheel yet.” She stood up. “If you don’t mind, I’m going to go hide my pathetic self in my bedroom for a while.”

As soon as she was gone, Jake dove across the room for Jane. He tackled her and kissed her. “You tried so hard not to want me. That's how I knew you'd never marry that weird Daniels kid." He kissed her on the mouth, again. "You don't have to try not to love people if you don't love them in the first place."

Jane wiggled out from under him. "Happy New Year, Jake."

Jane smiled at her class schedule, then folded it and slid it into her pocket. She had just dropped her French classes. Isaac had been right about that one—throwing French in on top of everything else she was studying added unnecessary extra work before graduation. Business degree with a side of criminal justice. She could get that done by spring.

She sipped her Coke. Spring seemed a long, long way off.

Jake tapped his phone and frowned.

They both shivered in their winter coats. The Portland State University Park blocks with bare tree branches creating a lacework above the statuary were romantic, even in winter, but not warm. He tucked his phone in his pocket and took her hand.

"So Jane, we've been officially a thing for twelve days now."

"Yikes. How did I forget that anniversary?" Jane laughed.

Jake stole a sip of her drink. "I want you to dump me. Don't interrupt."

"Yeah, I wanted to hear where you were going with that one."

"I want you to dump me the minute you don't think you would want me for your husband. I am all in on this thing, you understand that, right?"

"You've mentioned it." Jane took her cup back. Her parents were still mad that she hadn't come home for Christmas. She wasn't sure how she was going to explain the sudden switch from probably-going-to-marry-Isaac to…She smiled. It was too soon to even think that.

"I'm not fooling around. I'm pretty sure you understand the pressure I'm under with the business right now. With the mayor of Maywood breathing down my neck and the Fro-Yo Murder thing sending all my customers scurrying to Bubble-Bubble Tea, I can't have a flakey girlfriend thing, too. I don't mean you have to say that you're going to marry me this minute or anything. But if God starts talking, and he says 'No,' don't try and force it. Just dump me."

She chewed the end of her straw. Each season she seemed to be learning something else hateful about herself. She was too proud, she hadn't actually heard God's call to Kazakhstan, and now…she was forced to face the fact that she was really, really immature when it came to relationships. But now that she knew it, like the missions thing, she had to take it seriously. She couldn't go when God told her to wait, and she couldn't up and commit to Jake the same minute God had pointed out that she wasn't any more mature about boys than she had been at thirteen.

"Well?" Jake waited, his face slowly draining of all color.

"I promise. If God says to dump your sorry self, I'll do it."

"Or," Jake said, "even if it's not God. But if you realize you don't want me…"

Jane laced her fingers through his. "It's been twelve whole days, and that's not been a problem yet."

"So I think until that day—which will never come—we need to take this seriously."

"Sure." Jane squeezed his hand, but didn't make eye contact. She would agree to anything if she made eye contact, and that didn't feel wise.

"We should start making plans—"

Jane's phone jangled, so she answered it, relief washing over her. "Gemma?"

"Turn your radio on."

"What station?"

"Any! This is big news."

"I'm at school, I don't have a radio."

"Then hang up and find it on your phone. You won't be sorry." Gemma hung up.

Jane pulled up the local radio news.

"Just a second." Jake put his hand over her phone. "This is kind of a big deal."

Jane moved his hand. "Jake, I promise I will dump you the minute I realize I can't marry you. Please don't make that minute right now. I want to hear what the big deal on the radio is."

"There has been an arrest in the Fro-Yo Murder. Two men were arrested separately today. The detective in charge says that they were led to the two unrelated men by anonymous tips. Del Willis and Jason Miter are being held until their hearing. We'll give you the details as we learn them."

"Hey, good job, Detective." Jake held his hand up for a high five.

Jane stared at her phone. "Anonymous sources?" She looked at his hand, hanging in the air. "Oh, sorry."

He ran it through his hair. "Eh, no biggie."

"We were not anonymous sources. We were legitimate private investigators. Something tells me Detective Benedict is not going to be my inside contact with the police."

"Something tells *me* I'm going to have a long wait." Jake flopped back against the bench.

Jane smiled at him. "But it will be worth it, most likely." She picked up his hand and kissed his fingertips. "Unless I dump you, of course."

Now Available!

Chapter 1

JOSIAH MALACHI? REALLY?" Jane pulled her hair into a ponytail. The early spring day had been dry and hot for Portland—almost eighty. It was great for everyone's mood, but she felt sticky and dirty after her long bus ride home. She sat at the breakfast bar in her little apartment, the afternoon sun streaming through the partially closed blinds, and stared at her cousin in disbelief.

"Yes, really." Gemma leaned on the cracked, but clean, counter and checked her phone. "You can still come, if you want."

"But he's a quack." Jane checked her phone, too. Three texts from Jake Crawford, her boyfriend of the last four months, and one call from a client.

"He's not a doctor." Gemma tapped the corner of her phone in tune to the music coming from the other room. "Josiah Malachi is a well-respected and influential preacher. He even went on the Hallelujah tour with The Big Worship Band. This guy is hot right now. I'd bet most of the preachers in the world wish they were him."

"A church quack, then. You know what I mean." Jane stuck her phone in the pocket of her backpack. She needed to go for a run, and then call Jake back. Or maybe call Jake back and never, ever run.

It was a hard decision.

"Enlighten me." Gemma rested her chin in her hand. She batted her long black eyelashes in pseudo-naïveté.

"Health, wealth, prosperity. You too can be rich if you send me all your money. That kind of thing."

"The abundant life movement, you mean?" Gemma smiled. Condescension dripped from her words.

"Sure. Why not? The abundant life movement, where your hard work gives the preacher an abundant life." Jane glanced at the microwave clock. If she went for a run on this hot afternoon, she'd be proud of herself. If she didn't, she would have time to take a bubble bath before she went to Jake's.

"And so you don't tithe?"

"Gemma, you're just being difficult. Don't go spend your hard-earned money to see a health, wealth, and prosperity teacher." Jane didn't mention the half a month's rent Gemma still owed her. She cast a glance at the wall of kitchen cupboards, which she knew were empty.

"It's free." Gemma grinned.

"Don't spend your time, then."

"So stay home and watch soap operas with you?"

Jane wrinkled her nose. "*Downton Abbey* is not a soap opera."

Gemma lifted an eyebrow.

"It's not a bad one, anyway." Jane laughed. She felt light and happy at the thought of sitting around with Jake, snuggling on the couch, watching TiVo's episodes of *Downton Abbey*. A perfectly harmless, homelike evening. So normal it almost hurt.

Gemma snorted.

"It's better than bad theology."

"What's wrong with a God who wants to bless us all?"

"What about Paul? Being content no matter what your circumstances. The God I know isn't one who promises to make us all rich and healthy." Jane hopped off the stool. She couldn't run today and argue with her cousin. That much was for sure. But the argument didn't get her down. Gemma had always liked to push the boundaries of normal church life, and if Health, Wealth, and Prosperity was this week's new thing, at least Jane could be confident it too would pass.

"Would it be so wrong if he did?" Gemma unfolded the glossy Josiah Malachi leaflet.

"But he doesn't promise it." Jane scrunched her mouth in disgust.

"Yes, he does. And I'm tired of pretending he doesn't. And I'm tired of being broke."

Jane just shook her head.

"I'll see you tonight." Gemma stuffed the leaflet into her purse.

"Do me one favor while you're gone…every time he mentions a way you can donate to him, text me."

"Please." Gemma rolled her eyes.

"Okay, every time he says that your faith will make you rich, text me."

"Why not?" Gemma shrugged. "That's what I'm hoping he'll say, after all."

Jane and Jake played a game while they streamed the *Downton* rerun. Every time Gemma texted, they took a shot of espresso. Already Jane had horrific heartburn.

"What do you have against rich people, Jane?" Jake hopped off the arm of the aging velvet couch, wandered down the hall, and went halfway up the mahogany staircase. "They keep you employed and kiss you and stuff." His voice echoed through the house.

"I don't have anything against rich people." Jane was tempted to turn off her phone. One more shot and she'd have a migraine that would last a week. Even the usually comforting aroma of the rich coffee was making her stomach roil.

Jake took the stairs two at a time and disappeared into the kitchen. He came back in time to hear Jane's text alert.

"Don't do it." Jake put his hand over her small white ceramic cup. "Don't refill that."

"But…" Jane's hand shook as she reached for her espresso mug.

"Don't check the phone. Don't see if it was her." He pushed a plump blueberry bagel into Jane's hand. "Eat that or you're going to be sick."

Jane took a big bite of the sweet bagel.

"If you have another shot, I won't be responsible for my actions." Jake perched on the edge of the slate coffee table on his bare feet, like an acrobat poised to do an aerial flip.

Jane forced herself to swallow. "I don't know that you are responsible now. How much coffee did you have?"

"She's texted six times, plus I had some before you came over." Jake moved to the couch. He wrapped his arm around Jane. "But back to rich people. What's your real problem with this Malachi character?"

"You don't like this kind of thing either, do you? The televangelist, private-plane kind of thing?"

"That's not an answer to my question." He slid his arm down around her waist and tickled her. "Answer or I will torture you." His grin stretched from ear to ear.

"I am never playing an espresso shots game with you, ever again." She twisted away from his prodding fingers.

Jake pinned her, his knee pressing gently against her spine. "Is this better?" He moved his hands to her shoulders and rubbed them. "You are all knots. Did you work or something?"

"Yup. I had school all morning and then a house."

"If we got married…"

"I'd only have to clean up after you." She stretched her neck. "Right there. Yes! That's the spot." Jake's strong fingers worked at a knot right next to her shoulder blade. "When I'm living the life of luxury, I'm going to make regular appointments to see the masseuse."

"So, let me get this straight, please." Jake pressed hard against the knot.

A shiver of pain and relief shot up Jane's spine. "Oh, you're good!"

"Let me get this straight, I said. You are fine with marrying for money but not okay with praying for it?"

"That's the coffee talking, so I am going to forgive your nasty-minded comment." She rested her forehead against the silky arm of the couch.

"So you would still be into me even if I was broke?"

The phone chimed again.

"He must be closing up the show. That's a lot of comments about money in a row."

"Don't read it. And I need to know: would you love me if I was broke?"

"Of course. I'd probably love you better if you were broke. Being broke develops character."

"Good to know."

"Any reason you ask?"

"No reason." Jake kissed the back of her neck and then scooted away.

"Then can you unpause the show?" Jane reluctantly sat up.

Jake shut the laptop. "No, I don't think I will." He draped his arm over her shoulder and nudged her closer to him.

She turned around to kiss him, but her phone rang.

Jake answered it. "Love Shack, master of the house speaking." He held it to Jane's ear.

"Jane—he's dead—I—what do I do? I think it was murder!" Gemma's voice came through in ragged, broken sobs.

"What? Who?" Jane leaned forward. Her already over caffeinated and racing heart sped up.

"Josiah Malachi just died, right on stage. He just, he just…he's dead."

***

Health, Wealth and Murder is available now!

Don't want to miss the next Plain Jane mystery?
Sign up for the newsletter at TraciHilton.com to keep informed on all Traci Tyne Hilton freebies and new releases!

About the Author

When not writing, Traci accompanies her mandolin-playing husband on the spoons and knits socks.

She is the author of the Tillgiven Romantic Mysteries, the Plain Jane Mystery Series, the Mitzy Neuhaus Mysteries, and *Hearts to God,* a Christian historical romance novella. She was the Mystery/Suspense Category winner for the 2012 Christian Writers of the West Phoenix Rattler Contest and has a Drammy from the Portland Civic Theatre Guild. Traci served as the vice president of the Portland chapter of the American Christian Fiction Writers Association.

Traci earned a degree in history from Portland State University and still lives in the rainiest part of the Pacific Northwest with her husband, their two daughters, and their dogs, Dr. Watson and Archie.

Traci's photo by Jessie Kirk Photography.

Find all Traci's books and sign up for her newsletter at TraciHilton.com.

Connect with Traci at Facebook.com/TraciTHilton or tracityne@hotmail.com.

CPSIA information can be obtained
at www.ICGtesting.com
Printed in the USA
BVOW08s1347280217
477374BV00001B/19/P

9 781502 981653